Gwyneth Rees is half Welsh and half English and grew up in Scotland. She went to Glasgow University and qualified as a doctor in 1990. She is a child and adolescent psychiatrist but has now stopped practising so that she can write full-time. She is the author of *Mermaid Magic, Fairy Dust, Fairy Treasure, Fairy Dreams, Cosmo and the Magic Sneeze* and, for older readers, *The Mum Hunt, The Mum Detective* and *My Mum's from Planet Pluto*. She lives in London with her two cats.

The Mum Hunt won the Younger Novel category of the Red House Children's Book Award 2004.

Visit www.gwynethrees.com

Also by Gwyneth Rees

Mermaid Magic
Fairy Dust
Fairy Treasure
Fairy Dreams
Fairy Gold

For older readers

The Mum Hunt
The Mum Detective
The Mum Surprise
(for World Book Day 2006)
My Mum's from Planet Pluto
The Making of May

Cosmo and the Magic Sneeze

Gwyneth Rees

Illustrated by Samuel Hearn

MACMILLAN CHILDREN'S BOOKS

First published 2004 by Macmillan Children's Books

This edition published 2005 by Macmillan Children's Books
a division of Macmillan Publishers Limited
20 New Wharf Road, London N1 9RR
Basingstoke and Oxford
www.panmacmillan.com

Associated companies throughout the world

ISBN-13: 978-0-330-43729-5
ISBN-10: 0-330-43729-1

9 8

A CIP catalogue record for this book is available from
the British Library.

Typeset by Intype Libra Ltd
Printed and bound in Great Britain by Mackays of Chatham plc, Kent

This book is for my almost-nephew, Ethan,
with lots of love

I would like to acknowledge the input of the following people and cats: Sarah Davies, Alice Burden and the rest of the brilliant team at Macmillan Children's Books, Caroline Walsh, Polly Nolan, Rebecca McNally, Caroline Brown, Matthew Howard, the late (great) Tani Rees, Sooty Hyland and Matilda Rees, and the very present Magnus and Hattie Rees, Chloe Christie, Sparky Howard and the real Tigger-Louise.

1

Cosmo hated it when his mother gave him one of her really thorough washes. Her tongue was relentless as it cleaned his face, under his chin, the top of his head and even inside his ears. That bit was ticklish and Cosmo always wriggled, but his mother just placed her big white paw on top of him to stop him getting away.

Cosmo's mother was called India and she was a beautiful, pure white, short-haired cat with emerald-green eyes. Her great-great-great-grandmother had been a cat of a high pedigree flown to this country from India when her human family had moved here.

'Are there witch-cats in India too?' Cosmo asked her now, as India finished licking and moved back to inspect her work.

'Of course,' his mother answered. 'And in China and Africa and Australia and every other country in the world. Now sit there and keep clean until your father arrives. If I see you move from that spot, there'll be trouble.'

'I'm glad your ancestors came from India,' Cosmo chattered. 'Because it's such a beautiful name. It would have been awful if your ancestors came from a country with a *horrible* name, wouldn't it?'

His mother just smiled and said that if

2

they had then she wouldn't have been named after it.

'You'd have been named Snowie or something, wouldn't you, Mother?' Cosmo said. 'Like that white cat down the road.'

'I don't think I would *ever* have been named anything as common as that,' India replied. Sometimes she found herself sounding a little bit snobbish although she tried not to be. She was always having to remind herself that, just because she had pedigreed ancestors, it didn't make her any better than other cats, especially in this family, when all that mattered was whether you were a witch-cat or not. And she wasn't.

She looked at her six-month-old kitten with pride. Cosmo was nearly all black like his father, but had white paws and a white tip to his tail. Cosmo was her first kitten – an only one – and India thought him so

3

beautiful that it constantly surprised her that other cats in the street didn't stop to admire him more than they did.

Today was the day India had been dreading ever since Cosmo had been born. If only Cosmo's father, Mephisto, was an ordinary cat like her instead of belonging to a long line of witch-cats.

'Mother, tell me again what's going to happen today,' Cosmo said.

His mother tried to sound calm as she replied, 'You are to be tested to see if you are a witch-cat like your father or just an ordinary cat like me.' The witch-cat test involved mixing a drop of a special clear magic potion with a drop of kitten blood and seeing if the blood changed colour from red to green.

'I hope I'm a witch-cat!' Cosmo said enthusiastically. Witch-cats were different to

4

ordinary cats. Only witch-cats could assist witches with their spells and get to ride on a broomstick and do all the other exciting things Cosmo's father had told him about.

India hoped he was too, even though she had never liked the witch Mephisto worked with who was called Sybil.

It was a good thing to be a witch-cat though and, if Cosmo passed the test, India knew that Mephisto would be very proud and pleased. Witch-cats were becoming quite rare and difficult to get hold of and witches paid a lot of money to buy new ones. As well as helping generally in all witching activities, witch-cats were especially valued for their powerful sneezes. India hadn't noticed anything special about Cosmo's sneezes so far, but Mephisto had told her that didn't mean anything. A witch-cat sneeze was only magical if it was mixed with the other ingredients of a spell, and even then the sneeze of a kitten like Cosmo might not contain that much magic power. That was why the only true way to determine whether a kitten was going to turn into a witch-cat was to perform the special blood test.

India turned to look at the huge black cat entering their home through the gap in the garage door. Mephisto had the shiniest jet-black coat of any cat India had ever seen, and the darkest-green eyes. His big paws were twice the size of her delicate white ones. No wonder she had fallen in love with him when they'd met by the goldfish pond last year.

'So?' Mephisto asked Cosmo. 'Are you ready?'

Cosmo twitched his whiskers nervously. He greatly admired his father, but he was also very much in awe of him. Cosmo knew

how important it was that his father had a kitten who could follow in his footsteps, and he also knew he could only do that if he was a witch-cat.

Cosmo asked, 'Isn't Mother coming?'

India walked up to her son and gave him a last affectionate lick on top of his head. 'I'll see you later. I am not welcome in the witch's house. You know that.' India shivered at the thought of getting that close to Sybil. It was silly – and something that had caused a lot of arguments between herself and Mephisto – but there was just something about Sybil that made India's fur stand on end.

'Will *I* be welcome?' Cosmo asked, anxiously glancing across at his father. 'I've never been allowed inside before.'

'Today is different,' Mephisto said. 'Today is a special day. Come on. My mistress is waiting for us.'

Sybil was getting her witch-cat potion ready. That morning she had been to the special witches' section of the local supermarket to get some last-minute ingredients, and she was still wearing her human clothes. She decided it was time she got changed.

She went upstairs to her bedroom and took off the clothes she had stolen from various washing lines – she didn't see why she should have to *pay* for this disgusting human clothing – and stood looking at herself in the long mirror, admiring her green belly button and bright-green toenails and fingernails. She went to her wardrobe and flung open the door. She had already decided to wear a red outfit today. That way, if the kitten spilt any of its blood on her then it wouldn't show.

Sybil smiled when she heard a familiar *miaow* from downstairs. Mephisto was here. She knew she mustn't get her hopes up, because Mephisto's kitten had an ordinary cat for a mother, but she was hopeful that it would still pass the witch-cat test. She could do with another witch-cat to help her with her spells.

'Just coming, my precious!' she called downstairs to Mephisto. He was more precious than he knew, she thought. If it wasn't for Mephisto, Sybil wouldn't be able to operate her spells-and-potions business at all – though she made sure Mephisto never knew that.

Mephisto was waiting for her in the kitchen. He had originally belonged to Sybil's grandmother and had been inherited by Sybil when the old witch had died. Sybil had had an idea that she could breed from him and sell the kittens to make an enormous profit, but Mephisto had ruined her plan by going all potty over that stuck-up white cat in the garage. Sybil had wanted to get rid of India, but she hadn't quite dared. She had seen an item on the *Witch News* telling how, in some parts of the country, witch-cats were starting to select their owners rather than the other way round. Sybil wasn't prepared to risk upsetting Mephisto too much, though she doubted he had any new-fangled ideas of that sort since he still called her 'mistress' and believed that a witch-cat must always remain loyal to his witch, no matter what. Sybil had seen a film once about a butler who was so loyal to his master that he wouldn't give him up to the police even when it turned out he was a murderer. Mephisto was like that, Sybil thought. Though she wasn't quite sure how he'd react if he found out the truth about her.

Still . . . if she was careful, there was no reason why he *should* find out, was there?

Cosmo followed his father through the witch's cat flap. He was used to cat flaps, because his friend Mia, who lived next door, had one and she often invited him inside to

11

play. Mia's cat flap was see-through like a window, so you could peek into the kitchen from outside to check there were no humans about before entering. Sybil's cat flap had a cat-sized poster pasted on to it, which showed a cat being strangled by a pair of green hands. Mephisto had told him it was

just a deterrent to warn off strange cats, but Cosmo still got a fright every time he saw it.

Inside the kitchen Cosmo stayed on the doormat while Mephisto jumped up on to the kitchen table and miaowed his loudest miaow.

From the ground, the figure that entered the kitchen looked enormous. She was dressed entirely in bright red and her purple hair had rubber bats hanging from it. Rubber bats were quite popular with witches as hair accessories.

The witch beamed a big welcoming smile at the kitten. 'So,' she said in a loud voice. 'You are Mephisto's offspring!'

'What's an offspring?' Cosmo asked his father nervously.

'It's another name for a kitten,' Mephisto replied. 'Now hush! This is a very serious occasion.' Mephisto's eyes looked

13

different, Cosmo thought. Suddenly he realized that his father was nervous too – even though Mephisto was never normally afraid of anything.

'Well, Mephisto,' the witch addressed him, her dark eyes gleaming slightly. 'Are you ready to put your kitten to the test?'

'I am, mistress.'

'Then you know what to do.'

Sybil placed a rack containing two test tubes on the table beside Mephisto. One held a clear liquid. The other was empty. 'All I need is the final ingredient and the potion will be ready,' she said, shoving a pot of pepper in Mephisto's direction.

'What's the final ingredient?' Cosmo asked his father anxiously.

'A witch-cat sneeze,' Mephisto replied, leaning over the pepper pot and taking a deep breath. His black nose immediately

started twitching and he quickly placed it just above the test tube with the liquid inside. 'A-A-A-TISHOO!' he sneezed, and Cosmo could see little droplets of the sneeze falling into the tube.

'SPLENDID!' Sybil congratulated him as the liquid started to bubble and green smoke began wafting out from the top. She turned to Cosmo. 'Now, my pretty . . .' She had been saying that a lot since seeing *The Wizard of Oz* on television the previous Christmas. The wicked witch in that film was one of her favourite characters and Sybil loved the way she called everybody 'my pretty' and cackled loudly afterwards. Sybil had been trying to perfect the cackle too, but she wasn't very good at it yet. She pointed at Cosmo. 'Get up on the table and hold out your paw.'

2

With Mephisto standing next to him on the table, Cosmo held up his paw as Sybil approached them with a large needle. Cosmo began to tremble as his father licked the top of his head and told him to remain still, so it wouldn't hurt too much.

'Ouch!' Cosmo tried to pull his paw away, but Sybil held it firmly over the empty tube until the blood droplet she had drawn trickled down into it. Then she let go of Cosmo's paw and, using a glass pipette, sucked up some of her magic potion from the other tube and squirted it into the one with the kitten blood in it.

Cosmo was licking his hurt paw and not even looking at the test tubes when Mephisto said, 'Look! It's changing colour!'

17

Cosmo looked. Inside the glass tube his blood was changing from red to green.

'Look at the chart! Look at the chart!' Sybil cried out, holding the test tube against a shiny plastic-backed card on which were rectangles of different shades of green, from faint wishy-washy green, to medium green, right up to bright witch-green itself, which corresponded to one hundred per cent witch-cat.

Cosmo's blood was the same colour as one of the green rectangles towards the end of the row — only two shades less green than the brightest witch-green of all. 'He's eighty per cent pure,' Sybil screamed in delight. 'That means I've got another witch-cat! Ha! Ha!'

Cosmo looked at his father and saw that he was pleased, so he couldn't help feeling pleased too. But all the same, he didn't feel as excited as he'd expected. There was just something about Sybil that scared him.

'Where are you going?' Mephisto asked him, as Cosmo jumped down from the table.

'To tell Mother,' Cosmo replied, shooting out through the cat flap before his father could call him back.

*

India was at the goldfish pond where she was deep in conversation with Professor Felina. The professor was Mia's mother, who lived next door to them with a human called Amy. Professor Felina was a very clever tortoiseshell cat who was so studious that she rarely ventured outside. Felina was a professor of human behaviour – or Humanology as she liked to call it – and she had written several books on the subject.

'I didn't expect to see you this far away from your library,' India had said, when she came across the older cat staring down at the orange fish streaking about in the water.

'I've decided I need to start taking more exercise,' the professor replied, lifting her head and blinking her big amber eyes at India. 'I've been putting on weight and Amy has been buying in some sort of low-calorie cat-food. Of course I haven't touched it and she's feeding me boiled chicken now instead, but I am a little worried that I might be a trifle on the large side. What do you think?'

India had always thought that the professor was a rather plump cat, but she was far too polite to say so. 'Well, you do have a very thick coat compared to me, and that's bound to make you look fatter,' she said tactfully.

The two cats patted the water a bit together, but they were too busy talking to try very hard to catch a fish.

'How's Mia?' India asked. 'I heard that Amy decided to keep her as company for you.' Mia was Felina's only remaining kitten from her last litter. The other two had gone off to live with Amy's sister – also a great cat

21

lover – when they had reached the age of four months.

'Very well, thank you, though I'm worried she might not have inherited much of my intelligence. She really can be very silly at times.' Felina frowned.

'All kittens are silly,' India purred, thinking about her own. 'I wouldn't worry about it.'

'How is Cosmo?'

Now it was India's turn to frown as she told Felina about the witch-cat test and the bad feeling she had always had about Sybil.

Felina wasn't a witch-cat herself, but she knew all about the subject from her extensive reading. 'Well, *I* shouldn't worry too much about *that*, India. It's a documented fact that no witch can harm a cat. So if Cosmo *is* a witch-cat, he'll be perfectly safe with Sybil. Safer than he'd be with a lot of humans. It's all explained in one of my encyclopedias.'

India still looked worried, but at that point she heard Cosmo calling her. 'I'd

23

better go and find out what happened,' she sighed.

When India heard that Cosmo was a witch-cat, she was pleased for Mephisto's sake – until Mephisto announced that from now on Cosmo would have to live in Sybil's house with him instead of in the garage with her.

'But, Mephisto, surely he can still sleep here with me if he spends the day in Sybil's house with you?' India pleaded.

Mephisto shook his head. 'He needs to learn to be a witch-cat, by day *and* by night.'

Cosmo didn't want to move out of the garage either. He liked sleeping next to his mother on the old magic carpet that Sybil had dumped there because it had run out of magic. He also liked playing in the heap of old curtains that Sybil had thrown out when she had got new ones. He especially loved to watch his mother roll herself up in those curtains, pretending she was wearing a sari. With the red-and-gold material draped around her, Cosmo couldn't imagine even an Indian cat looking as beautiful as his mother did.

'But I always sleep curled up with Mother,' Cosmo said. Sometimes in the night he had scary dreams that made him twitch in his sleep, and his mother was always there if he woke up, with both her paws draped over him. She usually gave him a warm lick and told him a story to help him go back to sleep again. Cosmo couldn't imagine his father doing that.

But Mephisto would not budge on the subject, except to say that Cosmo could spend one last night in the garage with his mother. Then he left, saying that he would be back to

fetch Cosmo first thing in the morning.

'Don't worry,' India told him, when Mephisto had gone. 'I'm going to take you to see Professor Felina. She'll know what to do.'

Cosmo cheered up slightly when he heard that. He liked visiting his friend Mia. India led her kitten into the neighbouring garden and told him to hush as they approached Felina and Mia's cat flap. Inside, a soft human voice could be heard talking. India peered through the cat-flap window and could just make out Felina sitting at the head of the kitchen table, a plate of fish in front of her. Felina's chair was pulled up close to the table. Her back paws were on the chair while her front paws rested on either side of her plate. Mia was trying to maintain the same position on her side of the table, and Amy was sitting on her chair on the other side. All three seemed to be eating identical food.

India greatly admired the way Felina ran her household. Felina had the human Amy completely at her beck and call. Felina said it came from years of strict behavioural management, which basically consisted of

rewarding Amy's good behaviours and ignoring the bad ones. Felina was rewarding Amy now by fixing her lovingly with her big amber eyes and purring at her loudly between mouthfuls.

After the meal was finished, Amy dumped the dishes in the sink without rinsing them, just in case either cat wanted another lick of the fishy plates a bit later on. Then she went through to the front room to watch television.

India tapped the cat flap once to let Felina know she was there. The cat professor immediately miaowed for them to come inside.

Mia was excited to see her friend. 'I've made a great scratching post out of the bottom stair,' she told him, as India explained to Felina why they were there. 'Come and see!'

28

But Felina had other ideas. 'Before anyone goes off to play there is some learning to be done,' she said firmly.

Mia groaned. She hated that word. *Learning* was the thing her mother valued above everything else, but to Mia learning was just boring. So far her mother was teaching her to read and write cat language, to understand rudimentary human and dog language, and to play the piano by walking up and down on the keys. Mia really envied Cosmo, who got to play outside a lot more than she did and whose mother seemed to think that the only thing a kitten needed to learn was how to keep itself clean. Keeping yourself clean was pretty easy, Mia thought, especially if you were a tabby cat like she was, with no white bits to show up the dirt.

Felina led them upstairs to her study. (Amy was constantly surprised by how her

29

books seemed to multiply by themselves. If she had looked at them more often she would have been even more surprised to find that some of them were written in a strange language made up of different scratches.)

'So,' Felina repeated, starting to flick through one of her cat encyclopedias. 'You say Cosmo has passed the witch-cat test and Mephisto wants him to move in with Sybil . . .'

'That's right. Are you *sure* witches can't harm cats?' India asked her.

Felina had already laid the encyclopedia on the floor, and opened it at the letter W for Witch. There were lots of pictures in the book, which the kittens rushed forward to look at, but Felina miaowed at them to keep back. 'I don't want paw prints all over my lovely encyclopedia, thank you very much. Now, listen.' And she started to tell them a story.

'Long, long ago,' she began, 'humans and witches and cats and dogs and all the other creatures didn't exist like they do now. They only came to exist through a process called Evolution. Do you know what that is?'

Felina had taught Mia all about Evolution only the previous week, and thankfully she could still remember some of what had been said. (Her mother got very cross when she couldn't remember her lessons.) 'It's about when humans were apes,' she piped up. 'And cats were really big and scary.'

'Very good,' Felina purred, looking at her kitten in surprise. Maybe there was hope for her academic progress after all. 'But humans weren't the only ones who started

31

out as apes.' She flicked a page over and pointed with her paw to a picture of an ape-like creature with a green belly button and green fingernails and toenails, wearing a pointed hat made out of tree bark. 'That,' Felina said, 'is a Neanderthal witch.'

'A *what*?' Cosmo and Mia and India all miaowed together.

'An early type of witch,' Felina explained patiently. 'The difference between the prehistoric humans and the prehistoric witches was that the early witches befriended the cat species whereas the early humans didn't. When the apemen set traps, the ape-witches would warn our cat ancestors about the traps. In return, our cat ancestors helped the ape-witches with their spells. We know that one of the first things the earliest witches used their magic for, was to make a binding spell which bound them forever with the cat species so that no witch would ever be physically capable of harming a cat. If she tried then she went up in a puff of smoke. Look, there's a picture here of that happening.' She pointed to a colour illustration, which showed a witch stabbing a cat. In the next picture the same witch was turning into what looked like a large green smoke-cloud. 'In return for that, cats have always remained loyal to witches,' Felina finished, closing the book.

India listened to all of this in silence. She had never had a very scientific mind and she found it hard to understand how cats and humans and witches had developed in the way Felina had described. As for dogs . . . Well, she had always been told that they hadn't developed much at all from their primitive ancestors.

33

'Wow!' Cosmo miaowed. 'That's cool! But what about witch-cats? Where did they come from?'

'We have Evolution to thank for witch-cats too,' Felina went on. 'Some cats were better than others at assisting witches with their spells, and those cats became more and more closely associated with witches. After this had happened for generations and generations, two types of cat were created – witch-cats who had magic sneezes, and non-witch-cats who had ordinary sneezes. It's as simple as that.'

'Wow!' Cosmo exclaimed again. He didn't think it was simple at all. He looked at his mother to see how she was taking this new information.

India was looking a bit overwhelmed. 'I never considered myself particularly uneducated,' she said. 'But all this is news to me.'

35

Felina closed the book. 'You should learn to read, India,' she said a little sternly. 'All cats should learn to read and write. I keep saying this, but nobody will listen to me.'

'Mephisto says reading and writing is unnecessary,' India said, watching out of the corner of her eye as the two kittens headed off together to play a game behind the long curtains.

'Typical!' Felina scoffed. 'Fighting, catching mice and spraying your territory – those are the only things that matter to the male of our species!'

India smiled. 'Well, they are quite important things when your family lives in a garage,' she said. 'You're very lucky, Professor, to live in a house like this, with a human who really cares about you.'

'Luck had nothing to do with it!' Felina hissed. 'As I say to all my students, knowing how to select a good human at the outset is the most important thing any young cat can learn. You don't think I went up and purred at *every* human who came to the cat-rescue centre looking for a pet, do you? If you want a good home, you have to arrange it for yourself.'

But before India could reply, she was distracted by Cosmo, who was winding himself up in the curtain the way he had seen his mother do, but had got himself all twisted up. Mia was tugging at the material with her claws.

'Cosmo, stop struggling!' India miaowed. 'You're getting more caught up.'

Suddenly there were footsteps on the stairs and a human voice could be heard calling out Felina and Mia's names.

'Come on,' India whispered, unravelling the tangled curtain to free her kitten. 'Let's

37

go home. At least now I don't have to worry about you coming to any harm in Sybil's house, Cosmo, since we know that no witch can ever harm a cat.'

Cosmo didn't reply. He still thought Sybil was scary – even if she was a witch and theoretically more trustworthy than a human.

38

3

When Sybil woke up the next morning she was excited to see that some witch post had been delivered during the night. Every witch household had two posts – the ordinary one delivered by the human post-man every morning, and the witch post that was delivered during the night. Witch post was delivered down the extra chimney that each witch had added to her house when she moved in. Sybil's second chimney was purple in colour though, like all witch chimneys, it was painted with magic paint, so it was only visible to other witches.

Sybil picked up the letter. The postmark told her it had been sent by her mother, Euphemia. Euphemia was a very old and very evil witch who didn't have a very high opinion of her daughter, so it was most unusual for her to be sending Sybil a letter.

Before Sybil could open it, the bell rang and Sybil opened the door to find Bunty Two-Shoes standing there with a child Sybil didn't recognize. Bunty and her sister, Goody, were the joint heads of Witches Against Bad Spells, a society which closely monitored all spells-and-potions businesses, including Sybil's. All witches were capable of making spells and potions if they had a recipe to work from, but it was a bit like cooking – some witches couldn't be bothered or didn't have the time to spend slaving over a hot cauldron all day long and preferred the convenience of buying ready-made products. So Sybil had gone into business several years ago, selling spells and potions by mail-order catalogue.

Sybil despised Bunty, who reminded her

of the golden-haired Good Witch in *The Wizard of Oz*. Bunty didn't actually have golden hair, but she did have an angelic face (with cheerful blue eyes and rosy-red cheeks), which made Sybil irritated whenever she saw her. Bunty and her sister had already been responsible for banning her potion to make puppies' teeth fall out when it was put in their drinking water, and they had also ruined her plan to sell some spells that were past their sell-by-date to a blind witch who lived round the corner. Most annoyingly of all, Bunty's sister, Goody, had started encouraging witches to make potions that were totally organic, made out

41

of free-range frogs and toads (instead of the cheaper, mass-produced variety that were bred in captivity and never saw the light of day before ending up as an ingredient in a witch's recipe). Sybil didn't see the need to sell organic products at all, and she didn't care in the least what kind of life frogs and toads had before they ended up in her cauldron.

'Sybil, may we come in?' Bunty demanded crisply. She pointed to the child standing next to her, who had long, straight, dark hair and looked about nine or ten. 'This is my niece, Scarlett. She's staying with me at the moment.'

Sybil ignored the little girl. She couldn't stand children and if it wasn't against the law to invent a spell to do away with them, she would certainly be working on one. 'Hurry up then,' she snapped. 'What do you want?'

'A refund on behalf of Granny Brown,'

Bunty said, pulling a bottle out of her pocket, which had one of Sybil's unmistakable purple labels stuck on the side. Granny Brown was the oldest witch in the neighbourhood and was too frail to mix her own spells any longer. 'This potion you sold her has been watered down.'

'I don't believe it!' Sybil took the bottle from her, took it into the kitchen and tipped some out on to a saucer. It was very watered down indeed, a bit more obviously so than she had intended. 'I can't think how that can have happened,' she lied.

'I can,' Bunty replied curtly. 'You've been trying to cut costs again, haven't you?'

As Bunty and Sybil argued, Scarlett wandered out through the open back door into the garden, where Mephisto was giving Cosmo his first lesson on how to ride a broomstick. All broomsticks were made out

43

of a special type of wood that made them and anyone riding them invisible to the human eye, but Scarlett, being a witch, could see it. At the moment, the broomstick was hovering no more than a cat's height above the ground and Cosmo was perched on the stick, looking terrified, as Mephisto nudged it along gently from behind.

'Shouldn't you start him off with stabilizers on the back?' Scarlett called out to them. 'That's how my mother taught me to ride my first broomstick!'

Cosmo turned to look at her, lost his balance and tumbled to the ground.

Mephisto hissed impatiently. 'How many times do I have to tell you – you must *concentrate*!'

'It wasn't his fault!' said Scarlett, running over and sitting herself down on the grass beside them. 'Don't be cross with him.' She stroked Mephisto from his head right down to the tip of his tail. 'Wow! You're a really beautiful cat!'

Mephisto couldn't help purring slightly.

With her other hand, Scarlett tickled Cosmo on his tummy. Cosmo brought his back legs up to thump her, accidently scratching her because he hadn't yet learned how to play gently. He immediately rolled over and rubbed his head against her hand to try and make the scratch better. Scarlett laughed, stroking him on the head. 'Don't worry, it's just a little scratch. Anyway, it's my fault for tickling you.'

'Scarlett!' Her aunt was calling her.

'Got to go now. See you again, I hope!' she called back to the two cats.

'Come on,' Mephisto said, turning to his son. 'Let's try this again. One of our jobs is to deliver Sybil's spells and potions to her customers. To start with, you can ride with me. Then you'll be able to make deliveries on your own.'

'When will I get to help *make* a spell?' Cosmo asked eagerly.

'Later,' Mephisto answered firmly. 'Now get back up on to that broomstick. It's not really difficult. It's just like walking along the top of a garden fence. You can do that without losing your balance, can't you?'

'Yes, but a fence doesn't *move* while you're walking on it,' Cosmo pointed out, climbing back on again. 'Father, you won't let go, will you?'

'Not until you're ready,' Mephisto said. In fact, he had already let go, but he didn't tell Cosmo that.

As soon as Bunty had gone – with the promise that another bottle of potion from Sybil's new batch would be delivered to her that night so that she could inspect it before taking it to Granny Brown – Sybil tore open her letter.

Inside was a recipe, carefully written in green ink on black paper, with a note attached in her mother's spiky handwriting. This is what she read.

Dear Sybil,
Though you are not at all dear to me, I have just discovered a new, very evil, spell that only

you can help me with. You will see what I mean when you read the enclosed recipe. Nobody will be able to make this spell except you and I together, and so long as the ingredients are never discovered by anyone else, we should be able to become very rich indeed. Read the recipe and let me know if you think you can do your bit.

Your ever hopeful mother,

Euphemia

(Ever hopeful that you might not continue to be such a sorry excuse for a witch)

Sybil wasn't surprised by the unfriendliness of the letter. Her mother had always taken every opportunity to insult her. What surprised her was that Euphemia was requesting her help with something. Euphemia was a very powerful witch, and Sybil couldn't imagine what her mother could possibly need her help with.

She picked up the recipe and started to read it.

Mephisto and Cosmo were entering the kitchen as Sybil read down to one particular ingredient.

'I don't believe it,' she said out loud. Then she started to laugh. 'Of course! That's why she needs me!' She was so excited that she didn't even notice the cats in her rush to go across the road and show the recipe to her friend Doris. Doris was rather a dim witch (she preferred dogs to cats and owned a poodle) who never noticed when Sybil was horrible to her, which is what enabled the two of them to remain friends.

'Why is Sybil so excited?' Cosmo asked his father, but Mephisto's attention had been caught by something else. He was getting peckish and Sybil had left some

49

fillets of fish to defrost on the side.

'Come on,' he instructed Cosmo. 'Let's take these to your mother.'

The cat family were just tucking into their fish dinner when a loud miaow sounded outside the garage door. It was a miaow that could only belong to Jock, Doris's large ginger witch-cat with chewed ears, whose thick Scottish accent was unmistakable. He had been sent to Doris from a witch relative up in Scotland and he got on surprisingly well with her poodle.

Mephisto miaowed back, telling him to wait where he was. No other male cat was allowed inside his garage.

Jock miaowed something else that Mephisto couldn't understand. He found it very difficult to follow Jock's strong Scottish accent. When Mephisto went to the door,

Jock beckoned him to the garden. Mephisto followed him, feeling irritated. He hated to be interrupted in the middle of his dinner.

There was another cat already in the garden. It was Tigger-Louise, the tabby cat who was always hanging around with Jock. She lived in one of the big houses across the other side of the railway track with a young couple who had recently had a baby and constantly felt guilty for giving it more attention than their cat. Because of this, they were always trying to make up for their negligence by spending money on Tigger-Louise, who now had an expensive new collar made of black leather with fake diamond studs. Tigger-Louise was very proud of it indeed.

'What's wrong?' India asked, following Mephisto into the garden as Cosmo chased after her, trying to catch the end of her tail.

Jock said a sentence with lots of 'ochs' and 'ayes' in it, which India couldn't understand.

'Jock heard Sybil talking to Doris,' Tigger-Louise translated for them. Tigger-Louise had a better ear for accents than most cats on account of having travelled quite a bit with her humans. 'Sybil got a recipe for a new spell from her mother today, and Doris nearly had a fit when she read it. She said it was so evil that Sybil would be sent to witch prison if anyone found out about it.'

'What sort of spell is it?' India asked anxiously.

Jock couldn't tell them that because neither witch had said out loud what the spell actually did. But he was looking at Mephisto as if he really pitied him for having such an evil mistress.

Mephisto had heard enough. Any cat who insulted his mistress, insulted *him*. Besides, he wasn't going to be pitied by a scruffy ginger tom who came from a country where all the cats wore kilts. (Mephisto had never been to Scotland and he was rather ignorant about what it was really like there.) 'Did you actually *hear* this conversation yourself?' he demanded of Tigger-Louise, starting to growl.

'No, but Jock came and told me everything straight after.'

'And you can understand Jock perfectly, can you?'

'Well . . . not *perfectly*, but—'

'Exactly!' Mephisto spat out crossly. 'So this is a very unreliable second-hand account of what Sybil and Doris are meant to have said. I think you should check your facts, Tigger-Louise, before you go around spreading gossip!' Mephisto's tail was

53

starting to go bushy, which always happened when he lost his temper.

Tigger-Louise and Jock saw his tail and backed away.

'I can hardly believe that ginger tom is a witch-cat,' Mephisto hissed to India as they watched the other cats leave their garden. 'I can remember a time when no witch would *look* at a cat who wasn't jet black in colour. A ginger one would *really* be scraping the barrel!'

'Well, witch-cats are getting scarce,' India

reminded him. 'Witches can't afford to be so choosy any more.'

'*I'm* not jet black either, Father,' Cosmo piped up, lifting up one of his little white paws.

Mephisto turned on him. 'You're black enough!' he snarled. 'And who said *you* could leave the garage?'

Cosmo scurried back to finish his dinner as India whispered softly in Mephisto's ear, '*I* did, actually, dear.'

Mephisto growled loudly. '*I'm* the head of this family. Sometimes I think you forget that, India.' And just to show her who was boss, he lifted his tail and sprayed the area around them with his strongest scent.

55

4

India was worried. Mephisto might be too proud to entertain the idea that his mistress could do anything bad, but India thought differently. She knew one of Cosmo's tasks from now on would be to help Sybil with her spells and she didn't want him being part of something truly wicked. She decided to enlist Felina's help. If they could find the spell that Jock had been talking about, Felina would be able to read it and then they would know whether there was anything to worry about or not. India waited until Sybil and Mephisto went out to their weekly cats-and-witches coffee morning together, then she went to fetch the cat professor.

Ten minutes later, the two cats were cautiously head-butting their way through the cat flap into Sybil's house. Cosmo and Mia knew nothing of what their mothers were doing. They had been ordered to remain in the professor's study doing a lesson that involved studying a diagram of a dissected mouse and memorizing the names of all the inside parts, together with a rating of how tasty each individual portion was.

'I don't like the feel of this kitchen,' India said as she padded across the floor. She couldn't explain why but it made her shiver.

'There's nothing for *us* to be afraid of in a witch's kitchen,' Felina said firmly.

'I'm sure you're right,' India replied. 'But I still don't like it.'

Felina leaped up on to the nearest work surface. 'Let's check up here first.'

The two cats searched everywhere they could think of for the letter Sybil's mother

had sent. They even knocked over the rubbish bin and searched through that. India was starting to get anxious in case Sybil came back, when Felina called over to her, 'The thing we are looking for is a recipe, isn't it?'

'A spell recipe, yes,' India replied.

Felina was reading the letters on the front of a large flat book: R-E-C-I-P-E-S. 'This could be where she keeps it.' It was the sort of book with blank pages where you wrote or pasted in your own recipes. Felina started to nudge each page over with her nose, hissing as she gave her nose a paper-cut. Paper-cuts were a necessary hazard when you spent as much time with books as the professor cat did, but they still irritated her each time they happened. She turned the pages more carefully, studying each heading, until she came to the last recipe in the book.

A sheet of black paper was pasted on to

the page and the writing on the paper was in green ink. Felina tried to read the heading. She didn't immediately recognize the first word so she said each letter out loud, then tried to pronounce the word as best she could. '*Ee-youp-heem-ia*,' was how it sounded when she said it. Then she remembered that in human language, a 'p' and an 'h' together sounded like an 'f'. (She knew this from studying Mephisto's name.) '*Ee-you-fee-mia*,' she said.

'Euphemia! That's the name of Sybil's mother,' India said at once. 'That's it! That's the recipe we want!'

Felina went back and read the whole heading. 'EUPHEMIA'S SECRET RECIPE.'

'*Secret* recipe?' India repeated. 'That doesn't tell us much. Read the rest.'

But before Felina could start reading

the list of ingredients out loud, the cats heard the sound of a key in the lock and then Sybil's voice screeching, 'Don't park the broomstick there, Mephisto. Lock it in the garage.' Sybil had recently purchased a second broomstick − one of the latest models − and she was constantly afraid that it was going to get stolen.

'Quick!' India hissed. 'Out through the cat flap.'

When Sybil came into the kitchen it looked like a cat − or a very energetic kitten − had done a mad dash around the surfaces sending everything flying on to the floor, including her recipe book. The rubbish bin was knocked over and its contents were strewn all over the floor too. Sybil quickly picked up the recipe book and put it away in a drawer. It wouldn't do to leave that lying about.

Mephisto got an earful when he joined her in the kitchen. 'You'd better keep that kitten of yours under control if you don't want me to sell him to another witch!' she yelled at him.

Mephisto was surprised to see the mess and he couldn't help feeling a little proud of his kitten. It must have taken a lot of strength to knock over Sybil's bin like that. He spotted some chicken leftovers that Sybil had thrown in the bin the day before and started to drag a chicken bone with some nice fleshy bits left on it out through the cat flap, leaving a furious Sybil to clean up the floor.

Sybil couldn't afford to stay angry for long. She wanted to make up some potions that afternoon and she couldn't do it without Mephisto's help. All Sybil's spells required a lot of witch-cat magic, which is why she was pleased to have two witch-cats to help her now instead of just the one. So after she had calmed down, she called Cosmo and Mephisto into the house and didn't say a word about the raid on the kitchen. It didn't cross her mind that any other cat apart from her own could have done it as she knew all the neighbourhood cats were afraid to come anywhere near her.

That afternoon, Cosmo was going to help with his first spell and he was very excited about it. Sybil was using a shop-bought recipe book (written by a witch called Celia who had a cookery programme on Witch TV). Cosmo watched as Sybil opened a jar of frogs' legs, unscrewed a large bottle of sea water, and sniffed at the contents of a tin of rats' droppings to see if they smelt fresh. Lastly she went to fetch her bicycle pump, which contained some air that came from the top of a mountain in Wales. One by one she released the ingredients into her cauldron, and it started to bubble.

'Now, Mephisto, if you will just oblige with two of your finest hairballs and a

63

witch-cat sneeze, we will have everything we need. Oh ...' She beamed at Cosmo. '*You* are going to provide the sneeze today. I forgot.' She went to fetch the pepper pot, her eyes glinting greedily. 'I've got to give the proper potion to Bunty Two-Shoes, but for everybody else I'll water it down a little like I usually do. Then I'll put the price up, seeing as I've got two witch-cats to feed now.'

There were steps leading up one side of the cauldron and Cosmo watched as Mephisto mounted them, stopping at the top step to lean over the side. Each of the hairballs Mephisto coughed up seemed to make the liquid in the cauldron hiss and spit even more. Then Mephisto turned to him. 'It's your turn now. Make sure you sneeze over the cauldron, but don't let yourself fall in. I knew a witch-cat who did that once and it wasn't a pretty sight.'

Cosmo nervously climbed up the steps to join his father. There was lots of smoke and steam coming out of the cauldron and Cosmo was almost deafened by the loud bubbling noise. When Cosmo reached the top step, Mephisto grabbed the scruff of his neck with his teeth just to make *sure* he didn't fall in.

Sybil shoved the pepper pot under Cosmo's nose until it felt so itchy and tickly inside that he simply couldn't *not* sneeze.

'A-A-TISHOO!' he burst out, opening his eyes and watching sneeze droplets shower down into the cauldron.

To start with nothing happened. Then, as Cosmo watched, green sparks started to shoot up from the centre of the cauldron, then gold ones, then red stars, which shot up to the ceiling like rockets. The red stars banged as they reached the top and turned

65

into showers of red-and-gold dust. It was just like watching a firework display.

'There's nothing like a witch-cat sneeze mixed with the right ingredients!' Sybil crowed. 'I'm a genius! A genius!' And she started to dance around the kitchen.

Cosmo and Mephisto smiled at each other, thinking that they were both pretty clever as well.

The magic potion they had made was one of Celia's (the TV witch-chef) most popular recipes. It had recently been featured on Witch TV in a documentary about witch-cats. Celia's magic potion was said to have saved the lives of a huge number of witch-cats by stopping them being hit by cars. If the potion was rubbed on a cat's ears, it made the cat hear alarm bells ringing if it started to cross a road when a car was coming. The potion was expensive, but then so were

67

witch-cats, and it was becoming more and more in demand by witches who lived on busy roads.

'All I need to do is bottle it and do the labels,' Sybil said. 'Then, Mephisto, you can take some to Bunty before she comes round here making a nuisance of herself again.'

'Can I come with you?' Cosmo asked his father, thinking that he'd like to see the little girl called Scarlett again.

'If you think you can manage the broomstick ride,' Mephisto said. 'It's quite a long way. You'll have to sit in front of me and let me hold on to you really tightly.'

Cosmo's mother and father never bit him when they picked him up with their teeth by the scruff of his neck, but it wasn't very comfortable. Still, if he didn't let Mephisto hold him by the scruff, he wouldn't be allowed to go and he didn't want that. This would be his first proper broomstick ride.

'That's OK,' Cosmo agreed, quickly. 'When are we going?'

Cosmo was so excited as they set off that he almost forgot to wave a paw at his mother who was watching anxiously from the ground. He could see the Professor and Mia coming out into their garden to watch him too. He wondered if Mia wished she could fly as well. As Mephisto accelerated the broomstick upwards, Cosmo felt a funny lurching feeling in his tummy. They had barely passed over their own rooftop when he started to feel sick. The glass bottle with the potion inside was resting safely in the special delivery basket that Sybil had attached to the front of the broom, and Cosmo tried to keep his attention focused on that. But it was hard not to notice the chimneys and treetops and telegraph pylons and other tall things as they whizzed by, and it was also hard not to notice how far away they were from the ground.

'Father, I feel ill,' Cosmo gasped as his stomach gave another lurch and some foul-tasting liquid came up into the back of his throat.

Mephisto couldn't answer because he was gripping Cosmo tightly with his mouth.

'Are we nearly there?' Cosmo kept asking, terrified he was going to be sick all over Sybil's brand-new broomstick, but Mephisto just grunted and kept flying.

After they had flown for what seemed like forever, with Cosmo's stomach threatening to give up its contents at any minute, Cosmo glanced down – a big mistake – to see a little girl pointing up at him from her garden. As Mephisto brought the broomstick to an abrupt halt, Cosmo couldn't keep his stomach under control any longer. He was sick all over Sybil's shiny new broomstick, the basket and the bottle of potion,

11

which had been carefully wrapped in purple tissue paper and tied with a green ribbon. (Sybil was actually surprisingly artistic when it came to wrapping up her products.)

'It's travel-sickness,' Mephisto sighed, after they had landed. 'I had it when I was a kitten too. You'll get over it.' And then, because he started to remember how horrible travel-sickness had felt when *he* had experienced it all those years ago, he gave Cosmo a sympathetic lick on the top of his head.

The little girl in the garden turned out to be Scarlett. Bunty, who had seen them coming, came out of the house with a bucket of water to help clean up the broomstick and Cosmo. She said it didn't matter about the potion because it would be fine when she took off the packaging.

'Come inside and have some tea with

us,' she invited them. 'Or milk if you prefer. I've just switched on the television. Jet and I were about to watch the *Witch News*.' Every witch had a satellite dish attached to their house, which, though it looked like an ordinary one, provided them with all the worldwide witch channels. 'Jet will be pleased to see you,' she told Mephisto as he started to follow her. Mephisto and Bunty's black cat, Jet, were good friends.

Cosmo held back. He didn't want to go inside in case he was sick again. His mother had told him that it was very impolite to be sick on someone's carpet.

'I'll stay out here and look after him,' Scarlett said. 'I know how he feels. I'm all right on broomsticks now, but I used to only have to *look* at one and it made me want to throw up.'

As Cosmo lay on the grass being

stroked, the queasy feeling in his tummy gradually went away. He started to purr.

He closed his eyes and had almost fallen asleep when Bunty called out excitedly from the house, 'Come and see this, you two! Sybil's mother is on the news!'

5

A reporter from the *Witch News* was interviewing Euphemia in her front room, the walls of which were painted gold. Euphemia had bright-green hair – she believed witches should keep their natural colour rather than dyeing it – and she was dressed in a very traditional black gown. She also wore a pointed black fur hat, which had a fake frog pinned rather fetchingly to the brim.

'That hat looks like it's made out of black-cat fur,' Scarlett said, peering at it.

'It's fake, obviously,' her aunt told her sharply, looking apologetically at Mephisto and Jet in case they had been offended by the remark. 'No witch wears real fur – especially not cat fur.'

The reporter – whose green roots were

75

showing in his otherwise dark hair – was shoving a microphone in Euphemia's face and asking her if she had always been keen on gold.

'Yes,' Euphemia replied, showing her two rows of solid-gold teeth as she smiled. 'And as far as cats are concerned, I'd much rather have a gold one in my house, than a real one.' As she cackled, the camera moved across the room to show a gold statue of a cat sitting in the middle of her mantelpiece. The cat's face looked surprisingly lifelike.

'I thought all witches needed witch-cats,' Cosmo said.

'Most witches do,' Mephisto agreed. 'But Euphemia is so powerful that she doesn't need any help with her spells. That's why Euphemia gave me to Sybil when her mother – my previous mistress – died. Euphemia said that Sybil needed me more than she did.'

'I understand that this statue is one of a hundred solid-gold statues of cats that you are going to put on sale in your exhibition, which is due to open next week,' the *Witch News* reporter was saying.

'A hundred!' Bunty gasped in disbelief.

'I guess what all our viewers will be wondering,' the reporter continued, 'is how you came to own one hundred solid-gold cats.'

'Well, I didn't purchase them,' Euphemia said, pausing for dramatic effect.

'Stole them probably,' muttered Bunty.

'I *made* them!' Euphemia announced, showing off her gold teeth again as she beamed at the camera. 'Artistic talent runs in my family, you know.'

'*Rubbish!*' spat out Bunty. 'She could never have got hold of that much gold. Besides, she hasn't got any artistic talent.'

'And can you tell us how much gold went into making these works of art?' the reporter was asking now.

'You'd be surprised how little,' Euphemia said, giving a secretive smile.

The reporter cleared his throat. 'Finally . . . Is it true that after you sell all these statues you're going to be one of the richest witches in the world?'

'Once I've sold my statues, I'll happily tell you exactly how rich I am – so long as you don't expect me to hand out any of my money to one of those charities you television people are always banging on about.' She cackled again. 'Now, if you'll excuse me, I have to get on.' She pushed the *Witch News* reporter to one side and shoved her own face up close to the camera. 'Anyone who wants to order one of my statues ahead of the exhibition can email me.' She flashed up a green card with her email address on it and three prices of statues – small, medium and large. The statues were expensive, but not so expensive that a rich witch or human couldn't afford to buy one.

Bunty turned to the others, looking cross. 'She's up to no good. Just where did she get those gold cats?'

'Maybe she flew to Egypt on her broomstick and stole them from there,' Scarlett suggested. She had learned at school how the ancient Egyptians – being a very advanced civilization – had made statues of cats in order to honour them. 'Or maybe she stole a whole lot of gold from somewhere, melted it down—'

'I wonder . . .' Bunty interrupted thoughtfully. 'I wouldn't be surprised if the whole thing is a hoax. She's probably collecting the money in advance, when she

79

hasn't really got any more gold cats to sell.'

'But would people give her their money *before* she gave them a cat?' Scarlett asked. 'I mean, nobody trusts Euphemia, do they?'

'Nobody with any sense,' Bunty agreed. 'But a lot of people don't have any sense when it comes to parting with their money.'

Everyone in the room looked glum.

'Well, there's nothing *we* can do about it, is there?' Scarlett said, starting to get bored with talking about Euphemia. 'Come on, Cosmo. I want to show you Aunt Bunty's magic carpet. It's really cool.'

Scarlett took Cosmo to a room at the back of the house. It had two comfortable-looking sofas piled with cushions, and on the floor in front of the fireplace there was a patterned rug. 'That's just like the one in our garage!' Cosmo miaowed excitedly.

Scarlett couldn't understand what he

said, but she knew that *he* could understand *her*. 'The good thing about magic carpets is that they never run out of magic,' she told him. 'But the bad thing is that whenever a witch steps on one they rise up into the air – it's sort of an automatic reflex for them. Of course you can always tell it to go back down to the ground again or to fly off to wherever it is you want to go, but the thing is, if you tread on one by accident, you find yourself being lifted up when you don't expect it. Aunt Bunty got a nasty bump on her head last time that happened – she lost her balance and toppled right over. After that she tried hanging the carpet up on the wall when we weren't using it, but it got so used to being in that position that it kept tipping sideways instead of lying flat when we needed it to take us anywhere.'

Cosmo touched the edge of the carpet

cautiously with one paw, but nothing happened. Evidently magic carpets didn't respond to witch-cats – only to witches – but he thought Scarlett must be mistaken in saying that magic carpets couldn't ever run out of magic. Sybil's had and that was why she had dumped it in the garage.

'Watch!' Scarlett said, stepping carefully on to the carpet and standing on it with both legs slightly apart to balance herself. As if it sensed her presence, the carpet immediately started to rise off the ground, flapping slightly at the edges. 'It only does that if a witch stands on it,' Scarlett explained. 'Lots of humans have a magic carpet in their house and they never know because every time *they* stand on it, it just acts like an ordinary carpet.'

Cosmo had never seen a magic carpet actually flying before and he wanted to get on

board too. He jumped up on to the arm of the nearest sofa and leaped on to the hovering rug. Scarlett was sitting down on it now with her legs crossed in front of her. She let Cosmo sit on her lap. 'Let me know if you start to feel travel-sick,' she warned him. 'Aunt Bunty will have a fit if you throw up on this.'

But Cosmo didn't feel the least bit sick any more. Scarlett ordered the carpet to give

83

them a nice smooth ride to the ceiling and back, and Cosmo decided that it must have been Mephisto's driving – with all that speeding up and slowing down again – that had made him feel so queasy on the broomstick.

Cosmo wasn't sick on the way home – Mephisto made a big effort to drive carefully – but his stomach was much happier when they had landed.

India was waiting anxiously inside the garage door, and while Mephisto was seeing to the broomstick, Cosmo poured out all his news. 'Bunty's magic carpet looks just the same as ours!' he finished excitedly. Their carpet was almost identical to the one he had been riding on earlier, except for the fact that it was covered in white cat hairs where India had been rolling about on it.

'Cosmo, come and help me fetch supper,

84

please,' Mephisto said, giving India a quick sniff as he passed. Cosmo's father sniffed his mother a lot, Cosmo had noticed, especially when he hadn't seen her for a few hours.

'I'll look in Amy's bin first,' Mephisto told his kitten once they were outside. Since Sybil never put down enough food for all of them, Mephisto always took it upon himself to raid Amy's bin for the rest. (Amy frequently threw away perfectly good bits of chicken because Felina would rarely agree to eat anything but the breast.) 'You go and see what Sybil has put in our cat bowl.'

Cosmo obediently head-butted his way in through their cat flap, but before he reached the bowl in the corner he was distracted by the sound of Sybil talking on the phone in the hall. She was saying, 'Yes, Mother.'

Cosmo moved into the doorway to hear better.

85

'Yes, Mother,' Sybil said again.

Euphemia must be a very scary person to have as your mother, Cosmo thought, remembering her appearance on the *Witch News*.

'*Yes*, Mother,' Sybil said for a third time.

It reminded Cosmo of a day a few weeks back when India had miaowed out a string of orders about how he musn't roll in the dirt, musn't play in rubbish bins and musn't rub himself against fences that had just been painted. When he had started to miaow back lots of reasons why a kitten *couldn't* always avoid doing those things, India's whiskers had shot forward and she'd hissed, 'Cosmo, if you know what's good for you, you'll stop arguing with me and just say, "Yes, Mother"!'

He wondered if Sybil's mother was cross with her now.

'But . . .' Sybil was attempting to interrupt. 'But Mother . . . Yes, Mother, Yes, Mother, Of course, Mother . . . But . . .' Sybil's voice was beginning to sound quite weak. Then she blurted out in one long rush, 'But, Mother, I didn't realize you needed the spell so quickly! I'll go and get the ingredients straight away in that case. It's just the main ingredient I'm not sure about. I mean, how am I going to get hold of that many—?' She broke off abruptly as she noticed Cosmo sitting listening. She took off one of her red pointy-toed slippers and hurled it at him, shouting, 'Stop spying on me, you wretched cat, or I'll get my mother to turn you into a toad! She can do spells down the phone, you know! That's how powerful *she* is!'

Cosmo fled out through the cat flap, forgetting all about checking the cat bowl for food.

'Cosmo, what's wrong?' India asked, standing up as he flew in through the hole in the garage door with his tail bushed up at the end.

Cosmo told her what Sybil had said, and India immediately felt the fur on her own back starting to rise. 'How dare she threaten you?' she growled. 'I won't have it! I'm going to tell your father that he's got to do something about it or—'

'Mother, don't . . .' Cosmo interrupted, because he hated it when his parents argued, especially when it was about him. To distract her, he told her the rest of the conversation he had overheard – about how Sybil intended to go and fetch the ingredients for her spell straight away. 'It must be the spell that Euphemia sent her in the post, Mother – the one that Jock said was really evil!'

India's green eyes seemed to get larger.

89

She sat down again but she still looked alert.

'She said she didn't know how she was going to get hold of the main ingredient,' Cosmo added. 'What do you think it is, Mother?'

'I dread to think,' India replied. 'Something that no other witch would dream of putting in a spell, probably. Baby frogs, baby toads . . .' She shuddered. 'I just hope it isn't baby mice. I know that sometimes cats *have* to eat mice if the only other option is to starve, but I do hate the idea of killing them for any reason other than hunger – especially baby ones.' India was an unusual cat in that she disapproved of blood sports of any description.

Just then they heard Sybil's front door opening.

'Come on,' India growled quietly. 'Let's follow her.'

6

Sybil was going to the supermarket. She was wearing one of her shabbier human outfits and carrying a shiny green handbag on one arm.

India, whose white fur coat looked immaculate, led Cosmo along the street. They kept to the side of the pavement close to the hedge so that they could take cover if Sybil turned round to look behind her, and halted outside the main entrance to the supermarket as Sybil disappeared inside.

'We'd better use the other entrance,' India said. She knew that a cat would look out of place in the human part of the supermarket, and most likely some well-meaning human would think they were strays and call the RSPCA to have them taken away.

They slunk round the side of the huge building until they reached the back, where some men were unloading boxes from a lorry. The two cats dodged past them and headed for a large, sliding metal shutter, which looked quite ordinary until you touched it in a certain place with your paw, when it slid up to reveal a little entrance hall. From there you could take a lift down to the witches' supermarket, which was situated directly under the human one. (It could also be reached from the main store by stepping through an invisible gap between the fish counter and the meat counter and taking the witch-escalator down to the basement.)

Cosmo had never been in a supermarket before. When they stepped out of the lift, two witches were waiting to step in, both of them laden down with shopping. There was a notice-board just inside the shop on which were pinned three large notices in green ink.

NO DOGS.
SHOPLIFTERS WILL BE
PROSECUTED.
NO KITTENS UNLESS
ACCOMPANIED BY AN ADULT.

Cosmo couldn't read the words but the meaning of each notice was perfectly clear, because there was a picture illustrating each one. The last picture showed a kitten on its own with a big green cross drawn underneath it, and another kitten, with a green tick under it, holding its mother's paw. Cosmo nuzzled up closer to India to make it perfectly clear that he belonged with her. He was starting to think that supermarkets were quite scary places.

'OK, let's find Sybil,' India said. 'And don't touch anything.'

Cosmo felt too nervous to dream of touching anything, but that didn't stop him from having a good look as his mother led him up and down the aisles where witches and cats were doing their weekly shop.

'VISIT OUR FOOD AND DRINK SECTION!' a voice boomed out over the tannoy, making Cosmo jump. 'CHECK OUT OUR SPECIAL OFFERS ON EYE-OF-NEWT TEA, FROGSPAWN TAPIOCA AND SQUASHED-FLY BISCUITS!'

'It's the spell department we want,' India told him. 'I expect that's where Sybil is headed.'

The spell department made up a good half of the shop. It sold a few ready-made spells, but mostly the shelves were laden

94

with spell ingredients. As far as Cosmo could make out, the ingredients seemed to be divided up into solids, liquids and gases. In the section selling solids, Cosmo stared in amazement at all the things on display.

There were jars of pickled insects, tins of toenail clippings, spiders' webs wound round sticks, boxes of birds' feathers of every possible sort, tubes of snake venom, bags of assorted skin cells, pots of maggot paste, packets of squashed mosquitoes (with or without human blood), and many more items that Cosmo didn't have time to look at properly.

They passed the liquids next – rows and rows of bottles and glass jars – and Cosmo recognized some of the items Sybil had on her kitchen shelves at home, such as Loch Ness water, serpent saliva, donkey dribble and scented armpit sweat (they were running

95

out of that and he wondered if Sybil would remember to buy some more).

They spotted Sybil in the gases section, where a witch could hand in her own container and purchase wind refills of any description. Sybil was checking out the price of stinky dog-breath compared with polar bear burps, which were both on special offer. She handed over her empty bicycle pump and asked for it to be filled up with stinky dog-breath, then headed off towards the fresh-produce counter with its rows of dead mice, frogs, toads and shrews. (Whenever India passed that counter she always vowed to become a total vegetarian.)

'Hey, Cosmo!' somebody suddenly shouted.

Cosmo turned to see Scarlett waving to him from the children's lucky dip. The lucky dip contained an assortment of items selected by foxes from rubbish bins, each one wrapped in brown paper so you couldn't see what was inside. You paid fifty pence for a ticket, and if you were lucky you might get a very good spell ingredient in your parcel, though more often than not all that you pulled out was an old sock.

Sybil turned round as well when she heard Scarlett's voice, and the two cats only just managed to dodge behind a nearby stack of tins in time. Fortunately Sybil's attention was immediately taken up again by the shop assistant asking her if she wanted the frogs and toads wrapped up separately or together.

Scarlett mouthed, 'Sorry!' at the two cats as they crept out from behind the tins. Sybil was such a horrible witch, she thought, that it was no wonder her cats felt like they had to hide from her.

97

Sybil marched down the aisle towards the checkout, swinging a bag of frogs in one hand and a bag of toads in the other. She had left her trolley in the checkout queue to keep her place, which had made all the other witches in the queue very irritated. Sybil totally ignored Scarlett as she passed her – children didn't rate saying hello to as far as she was concerned – but just as she

was about to reclaim her trolley she remembered there was something she needed to buy in the kitchenware section.

India and Cosmo followed her there, taking care to keep well out of sight this time.

'I need the sharpest knife you've got,' Sybil barked at a nearby shop assistant. 'It has to be able to slice through the body of a small furry animal.'

'A rat or a mouse, you mean?' the shop assistant asked.

'*Something* like that,' Sybil giggled, and something about the way she was laughing made the fur on Cosmo's back stand on end.

The first thing Sybil did when she got home was rummage around in her shopping to find the chocolate she'd bought herself for a treat. Cosmo came in through the cat flap

to see her biting the head off a chocolate kitten. She laughed when she saw Cosmo and put the rest of the kitten in her mouth whole.

Cosmo turned his head away in disgust. He wished he didn't have to stay in the kitchen, but his mother had asked him to. She wanted him to try and find out what Sybil was putting in her recipe.

Cosmo watched Sybil lay out all her shopping on the table, then take out her recipe book and open it at the last page. She started to check off each ingredient against her shopping. 'Human toenail clippings – yes. Two Golden Delicious apples with worms inside – yes. Cobwebs – yes. Frogspawn – yes. Iguana skin cells – yes. Centipede legs – yes. One golden eagle feather – yes. Two tubs of gold paint – yes. Serpent spit – got that already. One jar of sunlight . . .' She picked up the jar, tutted in disapproval at the price, and banged it back down again. 'Four frogs – yes. Three and a half toads . . . Ah . . . I can try out my new knife . . .'

She noticed Cosmo sitting watching her, and he wondered if she was going to ask him to contribute a sneeze to her magic potion. But she didn't seem to need any witch-cat help at all today. Instead she screeched at him to get out.

Cosmo hurried back to the garage where his parents were lying stretched out together on the rug. India was giving Mephisto's ears a wash, but she stopped when her kitten came in. 'Well?' she asked him.

'Sybil's making a spell for sure,' Cosmo said, reeling off all the ingredients that he could remember.

India looked at Mephisto. 'Do those

101

ingredients mean anything to you?'

Mephisto shook his head. He had witnessed the making of many spells and potions in his life, but, as he pointed out now, witches were always coming up with new ones. 'It's good that she's finally making something without witch-cat help,' he

yawned. 'She's never done that before. Perhaps she's getting more confident.'

'Or more powerful,' India added, looking worried.

'It's good for a witch to be powerful, isn't it?' Cosmo said.

India sniffed. 'It's good for a *good* witch to be powerful – yes.'

'Sybil must be a good witch, otherwise Father wouldn't work for her,' Cosmo pointed out.

Both his parents gave him a fond look.

'I work *with* her, not *for* her,' Mephisto corrected him gently.

'Are you sure about that?' India murmured, speaking so close to his ear that the words tickled.

Mephisto gave her an irritated growl in reply.

*

103

After they had eaten supper (Mephisto hadn't found much in Amy's bin, but had got them some very juicy leftovers from the bins at the back of the Kentucky Fried Chicken shop), India went to visit Felina to wish her good luck for the important lecture she was giving the next day. Mephisto went off on his evening prowl around the block. Cosmo had been told to stay in the garage, but he started to feel more and more curious about Sybil's spell. She must have finished mixing it by now. Surely it wouldn't hurt to sneak inside the kitchen and take a peek.

Cosmo headed back to the house and stopped outside to listen at the cat flap. He could hear voices inside. Cautiously, he pushed the flap open halfway and peered through. Sybil was standing with her back to him. On the opposite side of the kitchen table there was another witch. Cosmo

104

gulped. The black cloak, green hair and wrinkled face were unmistakable. Then she opened her mouth to speak, and Cosmo saw the gold teeth. It was Euphemia.

'Well,' Euphemia was saying. 'Here it is – my own special ingredient. Even more powerful than a witch-cat sneeze. I made it myself with my very own sweat.' She cackled loudly and scarily in a way that witches only ever did in the privacy of their own homes.

Cosmo pushed himself further through the cat flap to see better. Euphemia had pulled a clear test tube with a stopper in it out of her bag and she was tipping it up against the light for Sybil to see. Trickling down the inside of the tube were several large beads of green sweat, each of which was surrounded by a golden glow.

'Not so fast!' Euphemia snapped,

105

snatching the bottle away as Sybil made an excited grab for it. 'Have you got what I told you to get?'

'Yes!' Sybil nodded nervously. 'At least, I'll have them by tomorrow. Six of them. It's all I could get to start with but—'

'SIX!' Euphemia roared. '*Six* isn't enough! We need a hundred!'

'I know, I know. I'm still coming up with a plan to get the rest, but I'll think of something. I may not be a powerful witch like you, Mother, but I *am* blessed with brainpower! How else could I have set up my spells-and-potions business when really . . .? Well . . . You know what I mean.'

Euphemia looked amused. 'I've never denied you had cunning, Sybil, even if you haven't got much else. Here!' She held out the bottle of magic sweat droplets.

Cosmo stayed where he was as the two witches went over to the cauldron, which was bubbling away in the kitchen fireplace. As Sybil added the droplets, the bubbling got noisier, then there was a hissing and sizzling and what sounded like a mini-explosion inside the pot. Golden smoke started to rise out of the cauldron, more and more of it, until the whole kitchen was so full of smoke

107

that Cosmo couldn't see anything else. He knew he was going to start coughing if he didn't get some fresh air and he hastily backed out into the garden where he sat taking deep breaths.

Cosmo waited nervously outside the cat flap, nudging it open with his nose every few minutes to check whether the kitchen had cleared of smoke. Eventually he judged that it was safe enough to go back in.

Over in the fireplace the cauldron was still bubbling away, and now that the smoke had cleared Cosmo could see yellow-coloured steam coming out of the top. Euphemia and Sybil were no longer in the room. Cosmo badly wanted to know what was inside that cauldron. He crept across the floor and carefully mounted the cat-steps that led up the side. When he reached the little platform where he had stood before, there was too much steam rising up to see the surface clearly. Some magic liquids were cold to the touch even though they gave off steam or smoke, but his father had warned him that if the liquid *was* a hot one, the steam from it could burn you just as badly as the liquid itself. Cosmo was leaning forward trying to judge the temperature better when Sybil entered the room.

'Hey!' she screeched.

He got such a fright that he lost his balance, toppled forward, and only just managed to stop himself falling right into the cauldron. He miaowed as his right paw touched the steam and he leaped down to the ground, feeling as if his paw was on fire. Sybil was shouting at him, but he wasn't taking in what she was saying as he dived between her legs and flew out through the cat flap.

109

His mother, who was crossing the garden on her way back from next door, thought that twenty dogs must be after him from the way he was running.

'I've burned my paw!' Cosmo wailed as he reached her.

'*Burned* it?' India repeated, looking down at his paw in disbelief.

Cosmo looked down too and saw why she was staring. He hissed with shock. The fur on his right paw wasn't white any more. It was a shiny, shimmering gold.

7

When they told Mephisto what had happened, he took Cosmo back straight away to see what Sybil could do about his paw. Cosmo was scared and didn't want to go back inside the witch's kitchen again, but his father insisted.

'You don't want a golden paw for the rest of your life, do you?' he said sternly. He had already had plenty to say on the subject of kittens who disobeyed their parents by going out on their own when they had been told to stay in the garage where it was safe, so Cosmo didn't dare to argue with him further.

Mephisto led the way into Sybil's house, where the witch was standing at the cooker stirring up some hot chocolate for her bedtime snack. She turned as Mephisto jumped up on to the kitchen table.

'Ah, Mephisto. You've brought him back, have you?' She went over to Cosmo, who had stayed just inside the cat flap, scooped him up and placed him on the table. Then she began to examine his paw. 'Well,' she said finally. 'It's only the fur that has changed colour. That's lucky. Probably because it only touched the steam and not the liquid. That spell of Mother's is very powerful. You shouldn't have been so nosy, Cosmo.'

'What does she mean – *only* the fur?' Cosmo asked, shuffling closer to his father.

113

Mephisto didn't reply. He started to miaow at Sybil, telling her that he wanted Cosmo's paw changed back to its normal colour at once.

'It's no use shouting at me like that, Mephisto,' Sybil said. 'It wasn't my fault! I don't know how to change it back again, so he'll just have to keep it like that.' She looked at the paw again, adding, 'It's not so bad. Quite pretty, really. You can be the cat with the golden paw, Cosmo!' For some reason, that seemed to really amuse her. She started humming a tune, then singing out, 'GOLD*FINGER*!' at the top of her voice, not very tunefully – it was the theme song to a James Bond movie she had seen recently on the television.

'I don't have fingers on my paw – I have toes,' Cosmo mewed, fighting back tears. 'It's not fair! All the other cats will laugh at me!'

Mephisto said, 'No, they won't,' but secretly he thought that they probably would. Ordinary cats were a little jealous of witch-cats, so if a spell went wrong for a change, it was only natural that they should feel a bit smug and amused by it.

'I hate you! You're a horrible witch!' Cosmo spat out, leaping down on to the floor. 'I'm moving back into the garage with Mother!'

Mephisto decided not to stop him doing that for one night, since he was so upset – but he would speak to him more firmly about his duties as a witch-cat (golden paw or no golden paw) the next day.

It was the first time Cosmo had been in serious trouble. Mephisto was furious with him, because the next morning when he came to fetch him, Cosmo flatly refused to

115

return to Sybil's house with his father.

'Cosmo's upset because he had a bad dream in the night,' India explained, doing her best to defend him.

'I dreamed I fell into Sybil's cauldron and when I came out, I was a frog,' Cosmo mewed. 'Then I fell in again and when I came out I was a mouse and you started to chase me! I'm scared, Father. I don't want to be a witch-cat after all.'

'It's not a case of choosing, or not choosing to be one,' Mephisto answered impatiently. 'You *are* one, and that's that!'

'But I don't have to act like one, do I? Not if I don't want to. And I *don't* want to. Being a witch-cat isn't good! It's horrid!'

That was too much for Mephisto. He lifted one of his big front paws and whacked Cosmo on the nose with it.

Cosmo cowered into a little bundle,

backing nearer to his mother.

'That's no way to speak to your father, Cosmo,' India said sternly, but she moved forward to make sure Mephisto didn't try and hit her kitten a second time. 'Perhaps if you both calmed down a little, that would help,' she suggested.

Mephisto glared at her. Cosmo saw his opportunity and ran full tilt for the hole in the garage door.

'Come back!' Mephisto growled, but India stopped him going after Cosmo by laying a patient white paw on one of his black ones.

'He's like you,' she said, purring softly to calm him. 'He needs time to think about things before he sees the sense in them.'

Mephisto looked at her sharply because he wasn't sure whether that was an

117

insult or not, but she was looking at him so affectionately that he decided it couldn't be.

Outside, Cosmo didn't know that his parents had decided not to give chase. He bounded round to Mia's house and stuck his head through her cat flap. She was having a drink of water from her bowl and the noise of the flap opening made her jump.

'Cosmo, what's wrong?' Then she spotted his paw. 'WOW! How did you do that?'

Cosmo told her. Mia was very sympathetic and said she thought him very brave to have gone into the witch's kitchen and looked into the cauldron like that all on his own. 'I think you must be very brave just to *live* in that house!' she added. 'All the other cats round here are really scared of Sybil.'

'That's just silly,' Cosmo said, though secretly he only half thought it was silly now. 'I'm running away! Do you want to come with me?'

Mia, who thought that running away sounded preferable to staying in and attending the lecture her mother was giving later that day, mewed, 'All right. So long as we're back by night-time.'

Cosmo didn't point out that the whole point of running away was *not* to be back by night-time, just in case *he* changed his mind about that as well once it got dark.

As the two kittens set off together, Mia chattered excitedly. 'We'll have to catch a mouse to eat for dinner. I've never caught one before – have you?'

But Cosmo was still too upset about his paw and the fight he had had with his father to concentrate much on what she was saying. He was glad she was with him though. It would have been lonely running

119

away on his own.

'Look!' Mia suddenly said, after they had been following the pavement for a little while. 'If we cut through the garden of that house we can get to the field behind it.'

Cosmo let her lead the way and didn't notice that she was taking them very close to the back of the house. Suddenly they heard a frenzied barking and a huge Rottweiler dog with massive yellow teeth leaped out of its kennel just in front of them. It was tied up with a chain, but it could still reach them, and before Cosmo could do anything, it had grasped Mia between its massive jaws. Cosmo was too frightened to move. He was fixed to the spot, dizzy with terror as the dog dragged Mia inside its kennel to get a better grip on her. Mia was hissing and biting and clawing at it but it was twenty times her size and she didn't stand a chance.

Suddenly a loose piece of wood in the neighbouring fence was pushed back and a blue-eyed Siamese cat appeared, wanting to know what all the fuss was about.

'Help!' Cosmo cried out to her. 'That dog's got my friend!'

He didn't know what he expected the Siamese cat to do, but he certainly didn't expect what happened next. The cat moved right in front of the kennel and miaowed loudly at the dog, 'Put that kitten down at once!'

Even if the dog didn't understand cat language, it must have guessed from the Siamese's tone of voice what she was saying. And it was obviously afraid of her. It turned round, still holding Mia between its jaws, and dumped her on the ground.

Cosmo could hardly believe what he'd

121

just seen, but he didn't have time to ask the cat any questions, because Mia was obviously in a really bad way. She was unconscious, one of her front paws looked floppy and broken, and she was bleeding from several places.

'Come with me,' the Siamese ordered, picking Mia up by the scruff and carrying her through to her own property.

The Siamese took them inside her house and as soon as they stepped through the cat flap, Cosmo saw that this was a witch's house. A whole family of witches lived here by the looks of things, although none of them seemed to be at home at that moment. A massive cauldron sat in the fireplace, just like the one in Sybil's kitchen, and a child's broomstick with stabilizers attached to the back was propped up in one corner. There were some books of organic spells on a shelf near by, together with several jars of different

spell ingredients.

Cosmo watched nervously as the strange cat gently laid Mia down in her own basket. Then she jumped first on to the table, then up on to the shelf with all the ingredients.

From there she grabbed a bottle of pink-coloured liquid between her teeth and brought it back to where Cosmo was waiting. There was a stopper in the top and the Siamese told Cosmo to pull it out with his teeth while she held the bottle still.

Cosmo managed to wrench the cork out and then he watched as the other cat took the open bottle over to Mia and shook the

contents over her, circling round her the whole time until Mia's body was drenched in the pink liquid. Then the cat dropped the empty bottle, sniffed deeply at some of her own loose tummy hairs until her nose started to twitch, and let out a massive sneeze.

As the droplets of sneeze mixed with the liquid on Mia's skin, the air around Mia started to glow. It glowed first white, then red, then a pink colour like the liquid itself.

'The spell is healing her broken bones, stopping the bleeding and mending her torn muscles,' the Siamese explained, as Cosmo watched in awe. 'She'll be fully recovered when she wakes up.'

Cosmo was weak with relief. 'Thank you,' he gasped, over and over.

The adult cat walked over to her dish to take a drink of water.

'You're a witch-cat, aren't you?' Cosmo

125

said, watching her.

'That's right. My name is Tani,' the Siamese replied. 'Who are you and what are you doing here?'

'I'm Cosmo and that's my friend Mia. We were . . . We were running away . . . sort of.'

'Why?' asked Tani, casually licking her paw as she listened.

'So that I didn't have to be a witch-cat,' Cosmo said in a small voice.

'I see,' said Tani, looking like she didn't see at all, but had no intention of offering her services as some sort of counsellor about it. She yawned. She had been about to settle down for her nap when she had heard the noise from next door.

'Can all witch-cats do what you just did?' Cosmo asked.

'Yes. But a witch-cat has to learn which are the right spells and magic potions for each situation. We all need someone to teach us that before we can use our magic sneezes to full effect.'

Cosmo looked at Mia, who was still fast asleep in Tani's basket. He liked the idea of being able to make her better if anything bad ever happened to her again. Maybe it wasn't such a bad thing being a witch-cat after all. And the longer he sat in Tani's kitchen waiting for Mia to wake up, the more certain he was about what he was going to do. As soon as Mia was ready to go home, he would take her back and tell his father that he *did* want to follow in his footsteps after all.

They got back just in time for Professor Felina's lecture. Cats from all around the neighbourhood had arrived for it. The subject was 'Understanding Human Behaviour',

127

and it was being held in Amy's front room while she was out at work. The cat flap had been propped open in readiness, and Felina had knocked over the bag of dried cat-food, which Amy kept in the kitchen, to make sure that the floor was covered in enough crunchy-munchies to provide her audience with snacks.

Cosmo saw his parents sitting in the front row of cats, as Felina jumped up on top of the television, which she had decided to use as a platform from which to speak. The other adult cats – Cosmo and Mia were the only kittens – were starting to sit themselves down on the sofa. There were cats on the seat, the arms and along the back of it.

'That sofa's going to be really hairy when Amy comes home,' Mia whispered. She was fully recovered now and Cosmo could hardly believe she had been so badly injured only a few hours before.

'Will she be cross?' Cosmo asked, thinking that Sybil certainly would be.

'Yes – but Mother will go right up to her and lie on the floor at her feet and start purring very loudly. She always does that when Amy gets annoyed. Amy just gives in then and bends down and strokes her.'

'Your mother must be a really clever cat,' Cosmo murmured, finding himself a seat on the window ledge at the back of the room. 'Come and sit here. We can look out of the window then, if we get bored.'

Mia giggled that *he* was a very clever cat too.

Cosmo was glad that they had a view out of the window as the professor's talk went on and on and on. The grown-up cats seemed to be finding it fascinating. Even Mephisto, who had taken a lot of coaxing

129

from India to come, seemed to be listening attentively. The only two cats who weren't there were Jock and Tigger-Louise, who had stayed out in the kitchen chasing each other round the table legs like two kittens.

From the window, Cosmo had a view of Sybil's driveway. As he glanced out, he saw Sybil staggering up the drive carrying a large cardboard box. He immediately felt curious about what was inside. What if it was the secret ingredient for the spell Sybil was making? 'Come on,' he whispered to Mia, pointing at the witch with his gold paw, then putting it down self-consciously and pointing instead with his white one. 'Let's go and see what she's got.'

Mia was getting bored with her mother's lecture too, so she was happy to follow Cosmo. Jock miaowed something at them as they passed through the kitchen, but they

130

couldn't understand what he said.

Cosmo led the way to his own cat flap with Mia following close behind. When they got there he warned her that they would have to be very quiet if they didn't want Sybil to hear them and throw them out. 'She's making a really big secret of her new spell,' he explained. 'She won't even tell Father what it's for.'

He pushed the cat flap ajar and looked inside. He could see Sybil taking off her little-old-lady wig in the hall. 'Come on,' he said, leading the way inside. Sybil had already placed the cardboard box down on the kitchen table. 'Stay here,' he whispered to Mia. 'I'll jump up and see what's in that box.' But before he could, Sybil was marching back into the kitchen, shaking out her purple hair and looking determined. She didn't see Cosmo and Mia as they scuttled to hide in

131

the gap between the fridge and the washing machine.

'Now, my pretties,' she said, to whatever it was that was in the box and, as she opened it, a mewing sound came from inside. She put her hands into the box and pulled out a little grey kitten. Some more kittens of different colours put their heads up over the sides of the box and she pushed them back inside and shut the lid on them.

'She can't be going to use *them* in her spell,' Cosmo murmured, staring at Sybil in disbelief as she started to walk towards the bubbling cauldron with the struggling kitten in her hand.

But it looked as though she was.

'Cosmo, we've got to do something!' Mia cried out.

Cosmo sprang out of his hiding place, leaped up on to the nearest kitchen surface,

132

and jumped on to Sybil's shoulder, where he dug in his claws as hard as he could.

Sybil screamed and dropped the kitten – fortunately not into the pot – and fought like mad to detach Cosmo from her shoulder. On top of the table, Mia was trying to grasp the corner of one of the cardboard flaps of the box between her teeth in order to prise it

open. Just as Sybil grabbed Cosmo by the scruff and flung him across the kitchen, Mia succeeded in letting the kittens out. As Sybil rushed across the room to try and block their exit through the cat flap, Cosmo rushed after her, this time biting her ankle. She reached for an empty saucepan to bash him with and ended up bashing her own leg instead as the kittens escaped through the flap, nose-to-tail, one after the other.

Mia called to Cosmo from outside to hurry up and get out too, but Cosmo had fled behind the washing machine as Sybil threw a plate at him.

'I'd use *you* in my spell if it didn't mean depriving myself of a witch-cat!' she screamed at him, starting to drag the washing machine out of its space. Inch by inch it was moving forward. If she pulled it out completely, Cosmo would be a sitting target for Sybil to grab. Cosmo didn't believe any more that witches couldn't harm cats. Somehow, he thought, starting to panic, all those history books must have got it wrong.

Cosmo couldn't escape. The wall was behind him, with the fridge and a kitchen unit on either side. Sybil was in front of him, panting from the exertion of moving the washing machine, but still looking furious.

'Got you!' she shouted, reaching out and grabbing him.

And this time she did have him. She had him by the scruff and she was dangling him in front of her where his claws could do no damage.

Suddenly, Mephisto burst in through the cat flap, miaowing loudly.

Sybil instantly dropped Cosmo.

'Mephisto, thank goodness,' she gushed. 'I think I've given those poor little kittens a terrible fright. I was trying to do the witch-cat

test on them and Cosmo must have thought I was trying to murder them or something. He just went mad! I've picked him up to try and calm him down, but he still seems to think he has to fight me off with all claws.' She winced in pain as she gave her shoulder a rub.

Cosmo couldn't believe what he was

hearing. 'It's not true! She was going to use those kittens in her spell! She picked a kitten out of the box and took it over to her cauldron! She was going to drop it in!'

Sybil seemed to guess what he was saying. 'I suppose because I walked towards the cauldron to get my witch-cat test potion, which was just next to it, he must have thought I was going to . . .' She broke off and shuddered. 'But surely you've told him, Mephisto, that no witch can ever harm a cat? Why, I'd go up in a puff of smoke if I did!'

That seemed to be enough to satisfy Mephisto. 'Exactly!' he said to his son, whose exit he was blocking by sitting in front of the cat flap. 'You must have made a mistake, Cosmo.'

'Father, please let me out of here,' Cosmo cried out, and Mephisto saw that – mistake or not – his kitten was trembling.

Mephisto let Cosmo go through the flap first, then followed behind him. Outside in the garden, India, Professor Felina, Mia, Jock, Tigger-Louise and the six kittens were all waiting for them. India immediately rushed up and started to lick Cosmo all over, but in a comforting rather than a cleaning sort of way.

Mephisto told them Sybil's version of the story. Mia, who had rushed to fetch the adult cats when she realized that Cosmo was trapped in the house, protested that it wasn't true. She had seen Sybil take the kitten over to the cauldron too.

'I'm not saying you didn't see that,' Mephisto miaowed back. 'But she couldn't have been going to drop the kitten in. That would be harming it and if she harmed it, she wouldn't live to tell the tale.'

Felina said, 'I'm afraid that's true, Mia.

139

Remember what we read in the encyclopedia. No witch can harm a cat without destroying herself. It's a historical fact.'

'Oh . . . I'm *sick* of historical facts!' Mia hissed, running off towards her own house.

Cosmo, who had stopped trembling now, was trying to work out if he *could* have got it wrong. He remembered Sybil saying she'd use him in her spell if it didn't mean depriving herself of a witch-cat, but maybe she had only said that to give him a fright. He looked at the grey kitten. 'What did *you* think?' he asked it.

'I really thought she was going to put me in that cauldron,' the grey kitten mewed.

'Well, she wasn't,' Mephisto said firmly. 'Now, do any of you want to go back and let my mistress do the witch-cat blood test on you?'

Each kitten miaowed at the top of its

voice that it definitely did not.

'We'd better take you all back to the cats' home then,' Mephisto said briskly. (Apparently that was where Sybil had just got them from.)

The kittens looked relieved.

'You're such beautiful kittens that I'm sure some nice person will be along shortly to adopt you,' Felina told them, 'but you must be careful how you select your humans . . .' And she started to give them tips on how to act in order to get taken home by the human of their choice.

Cosmo and Mia hadn't told any of the grown-up cats what had happened to them that morning. They didn't want to get into trouble for running away. But Cosmo spoke to his father on his own as soon as he got the chance and told him that he did want to

141

be a witch-cat after all.

Mephisto didn't ask what had made him change his mind. He just looked pleased and told him that in that case he would take him out with him on the broomstick that night to help deliver Sybil's new catalogue to all the neighbouring witches. He promised to fly the broomstick very carefully and said that they could stop and take a break if Cosmo started to feel sick.

India, who thought that Cosmo taking a broomstick ride with his father was a good idea too, suggested Cosmo should have a nap and eat a good supper before he left. Tigger-Louise – who was used to travelling a lot with her humans in the back of their car – had advised her that a full stomach was the best thing for preventing travel-sickness.

By the time they were ready to go it was

dark. Mephisto said they would be riding by moonlight, which Cosmo thought sounded very exciting indeed.

It was a beautiful clear night and the stars seemed to be winking at them. Mephisto looked as if he was searching the sky for something as they flew.

'What are you looking for, Father?' Cosmo asked.

Cosmo was balancing more easily this time and Mephisto felt able to let go of him in order to answer. 'My birth star,' he replied. 'Every cat has a birth star – a star that was shining brighter than any of the other stars on the night it was born. Cats with the same birth star are often drawn together during life and, when they die, their spirits rise up to join the same star.'

'Wow!' Cosmo gazed up at the twinkling stars in awe, straining his head so far back to

143

look that he nearly lost his balance and fell
off the broomstick.

Mephisto grabbed on to him tightly

again – so tightly that he pinched his kitten's skin – but Cosmo didn't complain. He was really excited and he couldn't wait for them to land on their next rooftop so that he could ask his father to point out which star was *his*.

It took a long time to deliver all of Sybil's spells-and-potions catalogues down so many chimneys, but eventually they had only one catalogue remaining in the basket at the front of the broomstick. 'This one is for Bunty,' Mephisto said. 'We'll stop there and have a saucer of milk with Jet before we go home.'

Scarlett answered the door and was delighted to see Cosmo. Then she noticed his paw. 'What have you done to it? Come and look at this, Aunt Bunty! Cosmo's got a golden paw.'

Of course, Cosmo couldn't tell her how it had happened. It was a pity witches couldn't understand cats as well as cats

145

understood witches, Cosmo thought. He would have loved to have a proper conversation with Scarlett and tell her about seeing his birth star, which had turned out to be a big, bright-yellow one with a circle of smaller stars around it.

Scarlett was going into the kitchen to fetch some saucers of milk and Cosmo followed her.

'I'm sure Sybil must be a horrible witch to live with,' Scarlett chatted to him as she opened up the fridge. 'Mother and Aunt Bunty can't stand her. Aunt Bunty always feels guilty buying anything from her, but sometimes Sybil is the only one who has what she's looking for. Plus she knows that Jet likes to see Mephisto.'

Cosmo miaowed that *he* liked to see Scarlett too, so that was another reason to keep ordering things that needed delivering.

'I don't think there's anything Sybil doesn't stock,' Scarlett went on. 'Mum says even *she's* got to admit that Sybil's a very shrewd businesswoman.' After mentioning her mother again, Scarlett sighed. 'Mum and Dad are away at the moment, trying to find us a new home in the country. That's why I'm staying with Aunt Bunty. But I don't want to move out of the town. Mum says we've got to because our flat is too small and there aren't many witches' houses for sale here. Mum and Dad couldn't find one they liked anyway. I said, why couldn't we buy a human house here and convert it, but Mum and Dad want something we can move into straight away. Mum's going to have another baby next month – that's why we need more space.' Scarlett crossed her fingers for good luck. 'I hope it's a girl. I really fancy having a little sister.'

Cosmo realized then that what he and Scarlett had in common – at least until next month – was that he was an only kitten and she was an only child. It was lonely being an only kitten sometimes and he wondered if Scarlett felt the same.

Just then Bunty called to her niece to go and check the larder to see if they had any human wart shavings left, because if they didn't she was going to order some. 'It's impossible to water *those* down!' she added. 'So I might as well get them from Sybil.'

Cosmo followed Scarlett into the larder where Bunty kept all her spell ingredients. As Scarlett was looking for the right bottle, Cosmo leaped up on to the set of folding steps that Bunty used to reach the top shelves. From there he could see many of the same things that Sybil had in her cupboards at home. He touched one of them with his paw.

'You've spotted the witch-cat-test potion, have you?' Scarlett said, picking it up to let him have a closer look. There was a bottle next to it that looked very similar, which she lifted up too. 'This is the test they used on me when I was a baby,' she said. 'To see what percentage witch I was. I was ninety-nine per cent,' she added proudly. 'Mother and Aunt Bunty dug it out of the back of the cupboard the other day so they can test the new baby when it arrives. Even if both your parents are witches, you can still vary between seventy per cent and a hundred per cent. The most powerful witches are nearer the top end – like Mother and Aunt Bunty. Of course, *I'm* not all that powerful yet because I'm only a child, but I will be when I grow up.'

Cosmo hadn't even known that witches could be tested in the same way as cats. He suddenly remembered Sybil admitting that

she wasn't as powerful a witch as her mother, Euphemia. Perhaps *she* was one of the seventy-per-cent kind and that was why she needed extra witch-cat help with her spells.

Just then Bunty called out, 'Never mind the wart shavings now, Scarlett. Come and look at this!'

Scarlett and Cosmo went back into the living room where Bunty was flicking through Sybil's catalogue. She had stopped at the last page. 'Look!' She held it out to show Scarlett. 'Wait till I show this to your mother. She's convinced Euphemia is up to no good and now it looks like Sybil's got in on the act too.'

On the last page of the catalogue there was a special advert. Scarlett read it out loud. 'Beautiful ornamental cats for sale. Solid gold. Reasonable prices. Small, medium or large to suit mantelpiece, hearth or garden. Ten per cent discount if ordered through this catalogue. Order now while stocks last!' Scarlett looked at Cosmo. 'I hope she's not expecting *you* to deliver these to people,' she said. 'They'll be really heavy.'

But Cosmo wasn't worrying about that. He had just thought of something else, but it was such a crazy thought that he didn't dare say it out loud. In his head he was hearing the words Euphemia had used on the *Witch News* when she had been asked how much gold went into the making of her gold cats. *You'd be surprised how little*, she had said. And he remembered Sybil looking at his paw after it had turned golden and saying, *It's only the fur*, as if she had half expected it to be more than that which had changed. He remembered too how sure he had been that Sybil was going to drop that grey kitten into the cauldron. So what if . . . ?

151

But he knew that was impossible. It was impossible because witches couldn't harm cats – not unless they wanted to go up in a puff of smoke. He gave his head a shake and tried to shift the crazy thought from his mind.

Next morning the thought was still there and Cosmo knew that it wouldn't go away on its own. Crazy or not, he was going to have to check out his idea about the golden cats once and for all. Hopefully he would find some proof – preferably proof that he was wrong – and then he could stop thinking about it.

Sybil had gone out straight after breakfast and Mephisto and India had left soon afterwards to spend one of their romantic mornings together at the goldfish pond. That meant Cosmo had the house to himself, so he decided to go next door and see if

Mia was free to come and help him.

Fortunately, Mia had been given a day off from studying and was allowed out to play. He told her that he wanted to find Euphemia's recipe – the one that had made his paw turn golden – and that he wanted her to try and read what was in it.

'I've only just started to learn some human words,' Mia warned him. 'I only know my name and address and a few other things Mother thought would be useful for me.'

'Let's just try,' Cosmo persisted.

The recipe book was lying on its side over by the cooker in Sybil's kitchen. Luckily, Sybil was always forgetting to put things away in their proper places. Cosmo jumped up and started to nudge the pages over with his nose like Felina always did. 'It's the last recipe,' he said. 'I saw that when she opened it the day she bought all the ingredients.' He

153

held the book open at the last page with his paw. 'Can you read anything?'

Mia studied the recipe for a long time. 'I know that's a word,' she said, pointing at one. And so is that. You can tell words because they have little gaps on the page on either side of them. It looks like some sort of list.'

'It'll be a list of ingredients,' Cosmo said. 'Look down it slowly. Can you read any of them?'

Mia shook her head. 'No . . . Oh!'

'Oh, *what?*'

'That one there looks like the start of our address – the bit that Mother says isn't really a word but a number.' She pointed to it. 'Our address is a hundred Green Lane and that looks like the "hundred" part. The next bit is different though.'

Cosmo remembered Euphemia's conversation with Sybil about the recipe. *We need a hundred*, she had said, when they'd been talking about the spell's main ingredient. So the word *after* 'hundred' must be the word he was looking for – the word that told him what the main ingredient was, like frogs or toads or . . . Cosmo pointed to it quickly. 'Do you think your mother could read that word?'

'Probably,' Mia said. 'But she won't come and do it now. She's busy getting ready for a

155

meeting at Tigger-Louise's house.'

Cosmo was thoughtful for a minute or two. 'Is that bag of cat crunchy-munchies in your kitchen still really easy to knock over?'

Mia nodded. 'There are still some on the floor from the other day. Why?'

'I'll show you in a minute. Listen, if I memorize this bit –' He pointed with his paw to the first letter of the word that came after 'hundred' – 'can you remember the next?'

Mia thought she could – especially as it was the middle letter of her own name – so the two kittens hurried back to Mia's house. Once they were inside the kitchen, Cosmo used his paw to push some of the little round cat biscuits that were still on the floor into the shape of the letter he had remembered. Then Mia very carefully tapped her biscuits into place next to Cosmo's.

'Come on,' Cosmo said, starting to get

excited as he saw how his plan might work. 'We'll finish it off and then we'll ask your mother to come and read it for us.'

They raced back to Sybil's house and found that the next two letters were the same, so Cosmo said he could remember both of those. Mia memorized one more. There were only two more letters left after that – one each for their final trip.

When they had added the last of the letters, they stood back for a minute to admire the complete human word they had made out of crunchy-munchies. Then they rushed upstairs to ask Felina to come down and read it.

Up in her study, the professor was closing her morning newspaper ready to go out. 'What is it?' she asked as they burst in on her. 'Tigger-Louise is just about to take me to meet her humans. Humans with new

157

babies need *especially* careful training.' She started to give her paw a lick where it had got covered in newsprint.

'Mother, we've made a word out of cat biscuits and we want you to read it for us,' Mia said breathlessly. 'It's in the kitchen.'

'You've made a *word*?' Felina looked surprised. 'Well, well, Mia. I wrote my own first word when I was only a little younger than you—'

'Yes, but I bet you knew what yours said,' Mia interrupted hastily before her mother's expectations could rise too high. 'We've only *copied* this one.'

'Where from?'

But Cosmo shook his head at his friend to warn her not to say too much just yet.

'Just from a book we found in Cosmo's house,' Mia said quickly as they led Felina downstairs.

Tigger-Louise had arrived in the kitchen while they were gone. She was licking her lips and washing her front paws, and Cosmo and Mia immediately looked down at the floor where they had left their crunchy-munchy word.

'Oh no!' Cosmo mewed. 'Tigger-Louise, did you just eat a word that was here?'

'A *word*?' Tigger-Louise looked genuinely mystified. 'What's that, my dear?' She started to head for Felina's water bowl. 'I'd better have a drink before we go – dried food always makes me thirsty.'

Felina looked sympathetically at Cosmo and Mia. 'Well, it looks as if you're going to have to copy out that word for me all over again, doesn't it? Never mind. Copying it out a second time will help you to learn it better.'

'I'm getting sick of letters,' Mia grumbled, when her mother was out of earshot.

159

'I know,' Cosmo sighed. 'But we have to find out what that spell ingredient is. Come on. Let's get on with it before Sybil gets back.'

But when they reached Sybil's kitchen, they found that she was already back. She was sitting at the table drawing something with coloured pencils on a large piece of white paper. It looked like she was making some sort of poster.

'It's no good,' Cosmo said, making a hasty backwards exit through the cat flap. 'We can't look at the recipe again while *she's* there.' His tail was bushing up in frustration.

'Never mind. We can always try again tomorrow,' Mia said.

Cosmo didn't reply. If he was right, he thought gloomily, then tomorrow might be too late.

Cosmo stared at the poster Sybil had pasted to the front gate. On it she had drawn a picture very like the one attached to the window of the cat flap, except that instead of showing a cat being strangled, it showed a cat being fed a fat, juicy pilchard.

Sybil came out of the house now, wearing her cutest little-old-lady outfit and carrying a megaphone. Cosmo couldn't think what she was going to do with it until he followed her out of the gate and down the street. As she walked along she lifted the megaphone

up to her mouth and shouted out a loud message.

'FREE PILCHARDS FOR ALL KITTENS AT NUMBER NINETY-EIGHT GREEN LANE. COME TO THE HOUSE WITH THE POSTER ON THE GATE AND COLLECT YOUR FREE PILCHARD. FIRST COME FIRST SERVED. THERE'S PLENTY FOR EVERYONE. BRING ALL YOUR FRIENDS!'

Cosmo couldn't believe what he was hearing. Sybil never gave out anything for free. What was she up to?

He followed her all around the neigh-bouring streets until she finally headed back home. When they got there, they found two or three kittens already waiting at the gate. Sybil gave them an encouraging smile. She really looked very friendly in her white bun and flowery old-lady dress.

'Hello, my dears. Some of you will have heard stories about how scary I am, but as you can see, those are just silly stories. I'm not really scary at all. I've got a special treat for you, which I'll just go and get ready, then I'll let you into my kitchen one by one and you can tuck in. They're lovely pilchards from my cousin who's a fisherman and he's sent them to me by helicopter, so they're extremely fresh and extra-specially tasty. Just wait there for now and make a nice queue.'

Before Cosmo could add that as far as he knew, Sybil didn't have a cousin who was a fisherman, Sybil had spotted him. She quickly scooped him up and carried him into

163

the house. 'I need you to help me, Cosmo, dear,' she said, while they were still in earshot of the kittens. As soon as she had slammed the front door she flung off her wig and dropped him on to the ground, adding, 'Just keep out of the way, you little pest!'

Cosmo headed straight for the cat flap, but he found that Sybil had set it on the special lock that allowed a cat to come in, but not to go out again. Just as he was wondering if he could force it open, the front doorbell rang and Sybil went to answer it.

'Doris!' Sybil didn't sound very pleased.

Doris sounded excited. 'I've just ordered the latest broomstick attachment from Broomsticks.com. I've printed out a picture to show you. Look. It's sort of like a mini-caravan with wings. I'll be able to—'

'How lovely,' interrupted Sybil, not sounding as if she thought it was lovely at all. 'Now if you'll excuse me, I've got things to do.'

'I just saw your sign. Why are you feeding all the neighbourhood kittens? I thought you didn't like kittens?' Doris didn't notice Cosmo slipping silently past her legs as she spoke.

'I have to get rid of some out-of-date pilchards!' Sybil said sharply, so intent on getting rid of Doris that she didn't notice Cosmo escaping either.

'But—' Doris didn't have time to reply because the door was swiftly slammed in her face.

Once he was outside, Cosmo bounded out on to the pavement where the queue of kittens had now grown to six. There were the two marmalade brothers from the corner house, the white kitten from down the road who had the mother called Snowie,

165

and three tabbies who he didn't recognize.

'Listen, all of you,' he gasped. 'This is a trick! Sybil's just trying to get you inside her house so she can use you in a spell she's making.' Cosmo was almost certain now that what Sybil was planning was very evil indeed.

'But witches can't harm cats,' the white kitten said. 'Your mother told my mother that the other day. Mother says *she'd* like to move in with a witch, because our human isn't very nice to us.'

'Witches usually only want witch-cats to live with them,' Cosmo replied impatiently, eager to get back to the subject of the danger they were in.

But that remark – which Cosmo hadn't meant to sound tactless – didn't go down too well amongst the kittens. None of them were witch-cats (at least, not as far as they knew). 'Are you saying we're not *good* enough to live with a witch?' one of the marmalade boys hissed.

And his brother mocked, 'At least we don't do spells that go wrong and leave us with paws that are the wrong colour!'

167

All the kittens laughed.

Cosmo felt himself getting hot with embarrassment and he tried to curl his gold paw underneath him so that it didn't show. His tail started to swish a bit, which it always did when he got angry, and he had to concentrate really hard on trying to keep it still. He didn't want the kittens to think he wanted a fight. He had to get them to believe that he was trying to help them. 'I don't understand either how Sybil can want to hurt you,' he said, 'but I know she hasn't got any pilchards for you!'

Just then Sybil opened the front door. Her white bun wig was back on, although it was looking a little lopsided. 'Doris!' she shouted to her friend, who had only just started to cross the street back to her own house. 'I'm sorry I lost my temper just now. My barrel of pilchards is in the garage and

I'll need some help carrying it into the kitchen. Be a dear and help me, will you?'

Doris beamed with the pleasure of feeling wanted again. 'You do have a very bad temper,' she pointed out, wagging her finger to admonish Sybil as she quickly went back across the road to join her.

Cosmo was stunned. As far as he knew there was nothing in the garage except junk.

'No pilchards, eh?' the white kitten piped up. 'I reckon Cosmo just wants to keep all those pilchards for himself!'

Sybil addressed the waiting kittens, thankfully failing to notice Cosmo hiding behind them, announcing, 'I won't *open* the barrel until at least a hundred kittens have arrived.'

'Quick, all of you,' said the white kitten, who seemed to have appointed himself as their leader. 'Go and round up as many others as you can. I'll keep your places at the front of the queue.'

Cosmo didn't know what to do. Then he had a sudden thought. The kittens wouldn't listen to him – they thought he was stuck-up because he was a witch-cat – but they might listen to Mia.

He found Mia in her back garden stalking a butterfly.

He quickly told her what was happening. 'But I'm sure Sybil can't really have any pilchards in the garage or Mother and I would have smelt them,' he finished.

'Is your mother there now?' Mia asked.

'No. She's gone out to the goldfish pond with Father. Do you think we should go and fetch them?'

'Let's go and see what Sybil's doing in the garage first.'

They found the garage doors wide open. Sybil and Doris were already inside. Doris was hanging back while Sybil marched over to an old barrel that was lying on its side in the corner, half hidden by some cardboard boxes. Sybil had to stand on the magic carpet to get to the barrel, and as usual it stayed completely flat. Cosmo thought that Scarlett must have been wrong when she said that magic carpets never ran out of

171

magic. This one must have done or it would have sensed Sybil was a witch – and reacted – as soon as she stood on it.

Doris moved forward. 'I don't understand,' she said. 'That's just an empty barrel.' But before she could say anything else she let out a shriek as the carpet – which she was also now standing on – gave a sharp jerk and lifted itself up off the ground with both witches still on it.

'Down, down!' Doris shouted, but the two witches had already lost their balance and were toppling over as the carpet brought them back to earth again. 'Why didn't you say it was a magic carpet?' Doris gasped, sitting on the floor, looking shocked. 'I thought it must be an ordinary one. Why didn't it move when *you* stood on it, Sybil?'

Sybil, who was picking herself up and

giving the carpet a little kick with the toe of her shoe, looked irritated. 'It doesn't work properly, that's why!' she grunted. 'I keep meaning to get rid of it. I'm going to have a car boot sale one of these days and see how much I can get for it. Now help me with this barrel, will you? Those kittens *think* it's full of pilchards and that's all that matters.'

'I still don't understand how a magic carpet can work for one witch and not another,' Doris continued, but Sybil ignored her, and since Doris could never be bothered to think very much about things that she didn't understand, she let the subject rest.

Cosmo and Mia stayed in the garage, wondering what to do next. Mia was very worried about what Sybil was going to do to the kittens once she had tricked them into coming inside her house. Cosmo was worried about that too, but he was also thinking about

173

Sybil and the magic carpet. If the carpet had reacted to Doris like that, then it must be working after all. And if it was working then it should have reacted when Sybil stood on it. It didn't make sense.

'I think we should follow the witches into the house and hear exactly what they're planning,' Mia said, standing up to lead the way. 'Then I'll go and speak to those kittens.'

Mia reached the cat flap first, pushed it open and slipped inside. She was getting bolder about entering Sybil's kitchen now, Cosmo noticed. As Cosmo followed her, he remembered something important. The cat flap was set to let you go in but not out. He immediately stopped moving forward, but it was too late. His tail had cleared the flap and it was already clicking shut behind him.

They were trapped.

*

Sybil and Doris were in the front room drinking tea. Doris was drinking eye-of-newt tea and Sybil was having a cup of herbal. Sybil was allergic to eye-of-newt and she only kept the tea in her house in case visitors came. Her mother in particular was especially partial to it. They had left the empty barrel in the kitchen, and Cosmo and Mia saw that a large chopping board and the sharp knife Sybil had bought in the supermarket were laid out on the table. In the fireplace, the cauldron was simmering away although no fire was alight beneath it. It had to be magic rather than heat that was making it simmer.

'Do you *really* think she was going to put those kittens from the cats' home in her cauldron?' Mia asked. 'I mean, we could have got it wrong, couldn't we? Maybe it

175

just *looked* like she was going to throw them in, like your father said.'

'Maybe . . .' Cosmo murmured. But he didn't sound convinced.

'I mean, if Mother is right, Sybil wouldn't be able to kill a kitten without killing herself, would she?'

'I know it doesn't make any sense,' Cosmo agreed.

In the other room, Doris was loudly saying, 'I've never heard of a witch being allergic to eye-of-newt tea before. Usually it's only humans who come out in a rash when they drink it.'

Suddenly Cosmo had a very scary thought indeed – a thought that would explain everything. But it was so scary and ridiculous that he didn't even dare tell Mia.

When the two witches came back into the kitchen, the kittens hid behind the washing machine. Cosmo continued to turn his new idea over and over in his mind.

'Are you sure you don't want to help me with my mother's spell, Doris?' Sybil was saying, letting out a teasing sort of laugh. 'I'm sure we could find you a little share in the profits if you wanted to take part.'

'It didn't sound safe when you showed me the recipe,' Doris replied nervously. 'My mother told me about a witch *her* mother knew, who flew into a temper and deliberately knocked her cat off her broomstick. As soon as the cat hit the ground and died, the witch disappeared in a green puff of smoke and her broomstick was left flying about the sky all on its own. Witches can't harm cats, Sybil. You know that!'

'Old witches' tales,' scoffed Sybil. 'Totally unreliable. *My* mother says that if I use her recipe, I'll be perfectly safe.'

177

'But Sybil . . . that recipe . . . it's . . .' Doris picked up Sybil's recipe book and the kittens heard the sound of pages being turned as she started to flick through it. Then they heard her say in a shaky voice, 'I just can't believe you're really going to use this!' Doris started to read out loud the part she couldn't believe *any* witch could *ever* use. '*Take one hundred kittens and chop some of them in half according to required statue size. To make a small gold statue you will need one kitten, for a large gold statue, two kittens, and for a medium-sized statue you will need one-and-a-half kittens.*'

'Hmm . . .' Sybil sounded thoughtful. 'I wonder if it's best to chop them lengthways or across the middle.'

She was interrupted by a loud retching sound coming from behind the washing machine.

'Come out of there, you little pest!' Sybil yelled, assuming it was Cosmo.

But it was Mia who had thrown up, and before Cosmo could stop her, she had panicked and made a dash for the cat flap.

'It's that kitten from next door,' Sybil gasped in surprise, catching Mia easily as she pushed in vain at the flap.

Cosmo forced himself to stay where he was, knowing that if Sybil caught him too he would have no chance to help his friend. He was trembling and not just because Sybil had Mia. He was also petrified because he knew now that what he'd suspected about Sybil was true. She *was* using kittens in her spell!

'What are you going to do with her?' Doris asked, keeping well out of the way of Mia's sharp claws as Sybil dangled her by the scruff.

179

'What do you think?' Sybil scoffed. '*You*
are going to be the first kit-
ten I turn into gold,'
she told Mia, who
was yowling now
and trying to bite
Sybil's hand.
'But for now
you can stay
in there.' And
she dropped
Mia inside the
empty barrel and
closed the lid on her. 'You'd
better leave now, Doris, if you don't want to
disappear in a puff of smoke yourself! And
remember – if you breathe a word about this
to anyone, I'll . . .' She made her voice sound
very sinister. 'I'll tell my mother.'

Doris went pale at the thought. She

knew that Euphemia was so ruthless and powerful that even Sybil sometimes felt afraid of her. 'Don't worry,' she gulped. 'I won't tell. I don't like kittens. I only like dogs. You don't have to worry about *me*.'

Sybil nearly told her about her spell to make puppies' teeth fall out, because it amused her to shock Doris, but on this occasion she decided not to. After all, what she needed now was for Doris to leave quickly, so that she could get on with her spell without any more delays.

As Sybil led Doris to the front door, Cosmo saw his chance to escape and get help. 'I'll come back and rescue you, I promise,' he whispered as he passed the barrel where he could hear Mia scratching away at the inside. He darted out into the hall as Sybil was opening the front door, waited until Sybil had stepped out after Doris to

181

inspect the gathering kittens, and slipped out silently behind her.

He hurried round the side of the house and made straight for the alleyway at the back that linked his garden with the others in the street. He knew where the goldfish pond was and that it should only take him a few minutes to get there. He would tell his parents about the recipe, and they would realize he had been right about Sybil after all. They would know what to do.

But when Cosmo arrived at the garden with the pond, he found that it was covered over with a thick green net. There was no sign of his mother or father.

Cosmo started to panic. Where could they be?

He hurried back to check inside the garage in case his parents had come back while he was out looking for them. By this time his heart was pounding really hard.

His parents weren't there, but Sybil had left the garage door open and her broomstick was lying on the floor just inside. Cosmo stared at it. He knew that any witch-cat could control a broomstick if it was taught how. He had seen what Mephisto had done to get the broomstick started and how his father had directed it while they were in the air. He had watched carefully, but he hadn't attempted to do it himself yet. He wasn't even sure if he *could* do it. But if he couldn't find his parents, then he had to fetch someone else to help – and the only person he could think of was a broomstick ride away.

Nervously, Cosmo padded over to the resting broom, which still had its basket for carrying potions attached to the front. Maybe if he sat in the basket he would feel

183

less scared about falling off. But he knew that he couldn't just climb aboard. A broomstick wasn't like a magic carpet. It didn't lift off the ground just because it sensed somebody was ready to ride it. Broomsticks had to be started up by igniting the bristles at the back. What Cosmo had to do now was summon up a really good sneeze.

There was a lot of dust in the garage and dust was good for making you sneeze. Cosmo went over to a particularly dusty corner and breathed in as deeply as he could. He soon felt his nose twitching. 'A-A-A...' he began, racing back to the broomstick as fast as he could. 'TISHOO!' he finished, sneezing little droplets all over the bristles. Straight away the end of the broom started to glow, turning first yellow, then orange, then a warm-red colour. Cosmo jumped into the basket and miaowed a command.

184

The broomstick responded to his voice, recognizing that the voice and magic sneeze came from the same cat, and rose off the ground and out through the garage doors with such a jolt that Cosmo immediately felt his stomach lurching.

Cosmo held on tightly with his claws as the broomstick rose upwards at a much steeper angle than it had done when Mephisto was steering. He closed his eyes and forced himself not to look down, because he knew that would only make him feel more sick.

But he also knew that no matter how sick or scared he felt, he had to keep going. He had to get help in time to save Mia.

10

Like all cats, Cosmo had an excellent sense of direction and he remembered the way to Bunty's house without too much trouble. At least, he assumed it was his instructions that were getting them there. The broomstick sometimes seemed to know which tree to turn left at, and which lamp-post to fly over, even before it was told.

They had just flown over the park with the six tall trees when Cosmo became aware of another broomstick in the sky. There was definitely a witch on board rather than a cat, and as it flew closer, Cosmo saw that it was Euphemia. She seemed to recognize either him or the broomstick, because she flew right up to him. Her black cloak was flapping out behind her and her black pointed hat was tilting to one side. Her green hair was pushed under her hat.

'You're Mephisto's kitten, aren't you?' Her gold teeth glinted at him in the sunlight.

Cosmo nodded and trembled at the same time. Euphemia was using cat language. There were a few very clever witches who had taught themselves the language of cats, but Cosmo hadn't guessed that Euphemia was one of them. Cosmo felt even more afraid of her now he knew that.

'And does your mistress know you are out taking a ride on her broomstick?'

Cosmo gulped. He wasn't used to lying. 'Yes,' he mewed.

'In that case, you won't mind me giving her a call to check,' Euphemia replied, reaching into the inside pocket of her black cloak and pulling out a mobile phone. She

started to punch in Sybil's number.

Cosmo was so frightened he could hardly speak. 'P-please,' he stammered, 'I'm only g-going to see my f-friend Jet.' Cosmo had been managing to control his broomstick-sickness until now, but he was suddenly feeling much queasier. The broomstick tipped sideways to avoid a

bird, and that was too much for Cosmo's stomach. With a terrible retching sound, he vomited all over Euphemia's mobile phone.

Euphemia screamed in disgust, dropped the phone, then realized what she'd done and dived downwards to catch it before it reached the ground.

Cosmo saw his chance to escape. 'Fly straight to Bunty's house as quick as you can,' he gasped, and the broomstick took off at top speed.

By the time Euphemia had caught her phone and wiped it clean on a leafy tree, Cosmo was a small speck in the distance. Euphemia could have chased after him – and caught him before he reached his destination – but she decided not to. She was on her way home, where she was expecting a visit from a rich witch who wanted to buy two of her largest gold cat statues. The witch had promised to bring the money round to Euphemia's house that day, and she didn't want to miss her.

'I'll teach that kitten a lesson later,' she murmured under her breath.

A few minutes later, Cosmo landed with a thud in Bunty's front garden, catching the end of his tail under the broomstick. It hurt so much that he hissed out loud, but there was no time to stop and try to lick it better. He hurried round to the back of the house where he knew Jet's cat flap was situated and miaowed a few times to let Jet know that he was there. When there was no reply, he continued inside, only just managing to stop himself hissing in pain again as the flap came down on the sore bit of his tail as he pushed his way through.

The kitchen was empty. So was the

room next door where they had all watched the *Witch News* together. Cosmo padded around the rest of the house and went upstairs, miaowing loudly, but there was no one there.

Just as he was starting to panic because he couldn't think what to do next, he heard a noise downstairs. Someone was coming in the back door. He raced down the stairs as fast as he could and met Scarlett as she was kicking off her shoes in the kitchen.

'Cosmo!' she gasped when she saw him. 'What are *you* doing here?'

Cosmo mewed at her frantically, but she didn't understand. What she did gather was that he was very upset about something.

'Aunt Bunty understands a little bit of cat language,' Scarlett told him. 'But she's just left to go and see a witch who called up in a state about something. Aunt Bunty is a witch counsellor and she sometimes goes out to people if they can't come and see her. I don't know when she'll be back.'

But Cosmo didn't have time to wait until Bunty got back. He had to get help for Mia and the other kittens now. He grabbed hold of the leg of Scarlett's jeans with his teeth and tried to tug her towards the door. He had seen Doris's poodle do that when he wanted Doris to take him for a walk. Cosmo had always thought it looked very silly and undignified, but now he was desperate enough to try anything.

'What is it, Cosmo? Do you want me to come outside and play with you?'

Cosmo released her jeans and gave his most urgent miaow. Surely nobody could mistake that for him wanting to play?

'I don't understand, Cosmo.'

Cosmo tried to think of a way of telling

her that the problem was Sybil. He looked around the kitchen. There on the table was Sybil's spells-and-potions catalogue, with a picture of Sybil herself on the back. He jumped up on to the table and mewed and mewed while digging his claws into the picture of Sybil, until Scarlett finally asked, 'Is it something to do with Sybil? Is that what you're trying to tell me?' Cosmo had seen how humans and witches

indicated 'yes', and now he nodded. Scarlett gasped in amazement, because she had never seen a cat nod before. 'Has Sybil done something to scare you?' Scarlett was frowning, trying to read Cosmo's expression.

Cosmo nodded even more furiously and started to tug Scarlett towards the door again. This time she went with him, picking up her shoes on the way. When Cosmo had led her as far as the broomstick he remembered that there was something in Bunty's house that he wanted to borrow. He wasn't sure how useful it was going to be, but he wanted to take it with them anyway.

He hurried back into the kitchen and trotted across the floor to the larder. He jumped up on to the set of steps and on to the nearest shelf. He carefully picked his way along it, managing not to knock anything over as he searched for, and suddenly

found, what he wanted. He lifted the little bottle between his teeth, jumped down to the floor and ran back outside, where Scarlett was waiting for him.

'Shall I hold that?' Scarlett offered, taking the potion bottle out of his mouth and looking curiously at the label. 'Why do you need this?' But of course, Cosmo couldn't tell her.

Scarlett swung one leg over the broomstick and waited for Cosmo to jump into the basket in the front. Then she said the spell that started up the broomstick and they were off. Whenever Sybil rode her broomstick she always took Mephisto with her and insisted that *he* start it up with a magic sneeze, Cosmo remembered now.

As they flew over a rooftop with a witch's pink chimney, Scarlett suddenly said, 'I should've left a note for Aunt Bunty. Now if she comes back, she won't know where I've

196

gone.' She touched her pocket and added, 'I've got my wand to protect me but it won't be much use against Sybil. Even a weak adult witch is more powerful than a child one.' She sounded worried and Cosmo hoped that he wasn't doing the wrong thing by taking her with him. But how else could he save Mia?

As they neared Sybil's house, they saw a long line of kittens stretching down the pavement and round the corner of Green Lane. Sybil's neighbours would think they were seeing things if they looked out of their windows. After all, whoever heard of cats forming queues? As they flew nearer, it was clear that the kittens themselves thought that queuing was pretty silly and they were starting to drop out of line and become a disorganized rabble instead. There was a lot of nipping and hissing going on as the kittens jostled for places at the front.

'What's going on?' Scarlett exclaimed as they landed on the pavement in front of the poster.

How Cosmo wished he could tell her. 'Has Sybil come out?' he asked a black kitten he had never seen before.

'Yes. She said she was about to open the pilchard barrel and she was going to invite us in one by one.' He looked at Cosmo with narrowed eyes. 'You should be at the back of the queue, shouldn't you, since you've just arrived?'

'I don't want any pilchards,' Cosmo said. 'When did she say she was going to start letting you into the house?'

'In about ten minutes' time. That was ten minutes ago.'

Cosmo led Scarlett round to the back of the house. There was a lot of gold steam

199

coming out of the kitchen, and Sybil had opened the back door to let some of it out. Sybil wasn't in the kitchen. All Cosmo could think of was rescuing Mia before the witch came back again. He led Scarlett inside. He couldn't hear any sounds coming from the barrel now, and when he miaowed to Mia that he was back, there was no reply. He leaped up on to the lid and started to claw at it, then jumped down again and looked up at Scarlett. Scarlett, seeming to know immediately what he wanted, put the potion bottle down on the table and went to help. It only took her a minute to prise the lid off the barrel.

But in that minute, Sybil walked back into the kitchen. She was dangling the white kitten from down the road by the scruff of his neck, and he was now beginning to wish that he hadn't bossed his way right to the front of the queue. Sybil shrieked as she saw Scarlett standing there – and let go of the kitten.

Scarlett, seeing that the barrel was empty, dropped the lid just before Sybil pointed a long green-nailed finger at her. Cosmo saw that Sybil's eyes had fixed on

Scarlett's with a glare that seemed to be freezing the younger witch to the spot.

Scarlett was paralysed with fear. At that moment she really thought that she was

201

going to die. She had been taught that if you looked away from an evil stare of an adult witch before the older witch released you from her gaze, you would be reduced to dust, and she didn't feel strong enough to hold Sybil's gaze for much longer. Her mother had told her that witch-against-witch magic was the darkest and most dangerous type there was. Now Scarlett was sure that she was about to see it in action for the first time.

'Give me your wand,' Sybil commanded, abruptly breaking their eye contact.

Trembling, Scarlett took out her wand – a portable one that folded up – and handed it to Sybil. 'My mother will find out if you hurt me,' she said as bravely as she could. 'I left a note at home. Aunt Bunty knew I was coming here with Cosmo.'

'I shall just have to tell her that you

never arrived then, won't I?' Sybil replied. She looked at the barrel. 'You seem small enough to fit in there until I decide what to do with you. Go on. Get in.'

Scarlett started to shake even more. Inside the barrel she would be very squashed indeed – she doubted she would be able to breathe properly once Sybil had put the lid on. 'Please,' she said hoarsely. 'Can't you just tie me up?'

'So that your little cat friend can chew through the rope and set you free?' Sybil laughed. 'No, my pretty . . . Into the barrel you go!' And she turned Scarlett's wand around and pointed it at her in a threatening manner.

Scarlett knew there was no use trying to argue any more. Then, just as she was climbing into the barrel, Cosmo started to sneeze. 'A-A-A . . .'

The two witches stared at him as he jumped on to the table in mid-sneeze and knocked over the glass potion bottle he had brought from Bunty's house. It broke as it landed on the floor, splashing its contents everywhere, including over Sybil's foot. Before Sybil could move away, Cosmo leaped down on to her foot and dug in his claws as hard as he could. '. . . TISHOO!'

Sybil screamed in pain and kicked him away immediately, but Cosmo had already drawn blood. The blood was mixing with the witch-test potion that had been in the bottle (fully activated now by the magic sneeze). Instead of turning green as soon as it touched the clear liquid of the potion, Sybil's blood was staying red.

Scarlett gasped in disbelief.

'What are you looking at?' Sybil

snapped, snatching up the piece of broken bottle with the label stuck to it. Her face went pale as she read it.

Scarlett was climbing out of the barrel now. 'Your blood hasn't turned green. That means it can't be witch blood – not even seventy per cent witch blood like Aunt Bunty thought. That means . . .' Scarlett paused, still hardly able to believe what she had seen. 'That means you can't be a witch at all!'

'Of course I'm a witch!' Sybil shouted angrily. 'Don't try and argue with me. You're only a child. I'm stronger than you!'

'I don't think so,' Scarlett said slowly, moving forward to take back her wand. Sybil tried to keep hold of it at first, but Scarlett started to recite a spell and Sybil looked afraid and dropped the wand into her hand at once.

205

Cosmo's head was spinning as everything that hadn't made sense to him came together in his mind: the magic carpet, the eye-of-newt tea, Sybil not being able to start up her own broomstick, the way she needed extra witch-cat help with her spells – and how she could harm cats without coming to any harm herself. It all made sense if Sybil wasn't really a witch!

Suddenly there was a loud ringing on the front doorbell and a stern, familiar voice called through the letter box. 'Sybil, are you in there? Open up at once!'

'Aunt Bunty!' Scarlett rushed to open the door.

Sybil made a dash to escape out the back, but Bunty had just sent all the waiting kittens round to the back of the house. All Sybil saw when she looked out of the door, was a sea of little furry bodies – with the bossy white kitten at the front of them – all miaowing furiously as they demanded to know where their pilchards were.

As Scarlett told her aunt what they had just witnessed, Bunty was flabbergasted. 'Are you sure?' she kept saying.

'Yes, and don't you see, Aunt Bunty? This explains why Sybil could kill all those kittens and not come to any harm herself!'

Bunty shuddered. 'Thank goodness you and Cosmo got here in time! But I still can't believe that Sybil has only been *pretending* to be one of us!'

Doris, who had come in the door behind Bunty, was listening with interest. The more Doris had thought about Sybil's plan, the more worried she had become that by not doing anything to stop it, she was indirectly harming those kittens herself – and she hadn't liked the idea of indirectly disappearing in a puff of green smoke! She had contacted the Witches Against Bad Spells Society, and Bunty had offered to come round to her house since Doris was too afraid to be seen visiting hers. Once there, Bunty had seen all the kittens out in the street, extracted the whole story from Doris, and come straight round to Sybil's house.

Doris pointed at Sybil now, starting to feel excited as lots of things began to make sense to her. '*That's* why you came out in a rash that time when I accidently gave you eye-of-newt tea!' she gushed. 'And remember that time when I saw the green nail polish in your bathroom? You told me you'd bought it to give to a human friend who wanted to look more like a witch. Was that nail polish really for *you*, then?'

Sybil glared at Doris as if she was the most stupid creature on the face of the planet. 'Of course it was for me! I don't *have* any human friends! I can't stand humans! My father was human and it's ruined my life!' And she started to sob – big, clear, human tears, not pale-green witches' ones like she had always longed to have.

'I think, Sybil,' Bunty said sternly, 'that you had better tell us everything.'

Cosmo was mewing loudly now, trying to get their attention.

Bunty turned to him. 'Cosmo, what is it?'

'Where's Mia?' Cosmo miaowed as slowly and clearly as he could, so that Bunty could understand.

Bunty translated the question to Sybil, who hiccuped and looked guiltily across at the cauldron billowing out its golden steam.

As Cosmo followed her gaze, his insides went icy cold. Had he and Scarlett arrived too late after all?

209

11

'Are you saying,' gulped Bunty, as Sybil led her over to the cauldron, 'that Cosmo's friend is in *there*?'

'She's just an ordinary kitten, not a witch-cat,' Sybil said – as if that should make everybody a lot less concerned that Sybil had just drowned her.

'Get her out right now!' Bunty commanded.

Sybil gulped. 'Well, she won't be quite the same as when she went in,' she warned them. She pulled a long green rubber glove over her hand and arm and plunged deep into the cauldron's golden liquid, which was actually cool to touch even though it looked like it was boiling. What she pulled out made Cosmo hiss with horror. The thing

that Sybil was holding was a cat, the same size as Mia, but instead of being alive it was a statue of solid gold.

At that moment Mephisto and India walked in through the door, having pushed their way through the middle of all the kittens. 'What's going on?' Mephisto demanded loudly.

'Sybil's . . .' Cosmo began, but he couldn't think of the right words to explain

the horrific thing that had happened. He pointed a trembling paw at the little statue, which Sybil had set down on the table.

Professor Felina, who had just got back from Tigger-Louise's and had also come to see what was going on, walked into the kitchen to join them. She looked at the gathering of cats and witches and asked, 'Where's Mia?'

'There!' Cosmo spat out, pointing at the statue, before Bunty had time to break the news more gently.

The professor stared at the gold statue for a long moment, looking stunned, then, for the first time in her life, she uttered the words, 'I don't understand.'

'I'm afraid Sybil has put Mia in her cauldron and turned her into gold,' Bunty said.

All three adult cats stared at her. 'But witches can't harm cats!' they chorused.

212

'Sybil isn't really a witch,' Cosmo
mewed. 'Her blood doesn't go green when
you test it. That's why she can kill cats without killing herself.'

Felina stayed so still that she too looked
almost like a statue for a moment. Then she
let out a strangled cry and jumped up on to
the table. Her whole body was trembling.
She started desperately to lick at the statue
as if she were trying to turn it back into
Mia.

It was too much for India, who could
imagine only too well how *she* would feel if
Cosmo had been the one who had been
turned into gold. 'Mephisto, can't you do
something?' she hissed, jumping up to stand
beside Felina who she attempted to comfort
by rubbing her head against her face.

'Only the witch who made the spell
knows if it can be undone again,' Mephisto

replied jerkily. He was still reeling from the information that his mistress was an imposter − not a true witch at all. How could he − one of the most respected and experienced witch-cats in the neighbourhood − have been fooled like that? It couldn't be true! It was impossible!

Bunty was angrily turning on Sybil. 'Tell us about this spell right now, Sybil!'

Sybil stuck out her chin stubbornly. 'Why should I? The same thing will happen to me if I tell you or if I don't!'

'Not necessarily!' Bunty snapped.

'What do you mean?'

'You'll go to prison, but not necessarily witch prison,' Bunty was watching Sybil's face closely. 'We might have to arrange for you to go to a human prison, since you are more human than witch.'

'No!' screeched Sybil. 'You can't do that!

214

I've lived as a witch all my life! I can't live amongst *humans*!' She said the last word as if it contained a bad smell.

'Well then,' Bunty said, settling herself comfortably on one of Sybil's kitchen chairs. 'You had better cooperate fully with us, hadn't you?'

And Sybil, under threat of being sent to a human prison, lost no time in telling them everything.

First she explained that, although she was Euphemia's daughter, her father had been human. 'He was a very bad human, but he was human just the same. Mother got rid of him soon after I was born – she says she can't see what attracted her to him in the first place, except maybe his badness.

Anyway, when my mother tested me she found that I took more after him than her and that I had less than the required

215

percentage of witch blood to make me a witch.

She was ashamed of me at first, but then she saw how determined I was to be thought of as a witch, and how clever I was, and how I could trick everybody into believing I was a witch when I wasn't. I used green polish for my nails and green paint for my belly button so that I looked just like any other witch, and I learned to balance on a broomstick if a witch-cat or my mother powered it up for me.

I lived at home with Mother for a long time, helping her with her spells. Then when my grandmother died my mother said I should have her cat – Mephisto – because she knew he was very powerful and would be able to help me a lot. It was then that I set up my own spells-and-potions business and used Mephisto's

216

sneezes to make them work. My mother carried on keeping my secret for me, although she always told me that one day she would ask me for something in return.' She paused.

Bunty said quietly, looking at the golden Mia, 'And now she has.'

Sybil nodded. 'Mother came across the spell by accident. She was mixing up some ingredients she'd never used before to try and make some magic paint. The back door was open and a nosy kitten from one of her neighbour's houses came inside. It jumped up on to the shelf above Mother's cauldron, slipped and fell right in. When Mother fished it out, she found that it had turned to solid gold. Mother loves gold, so she got very excited and—'

'I don't understand,' Scarlett interrupted. 'If Euphemia killed a cat – and she *is* a witch

217

– then why didn't she go up in a puff of smoke?'

'I expect the curse wasn't activated at that point, because she hadn't killed the kitten on purpose,' Bunty said. 'On that occasion, it really was a genuine accident.'

'That's right.' Sybil nodded. 'But after it had happened, it gave her an idea and she went to look up all her books on Dark Magic—'

'Books of evil spells,' Bunty explained quickly to Scarlett. 'It's against the law to own such books, but many bad witches still do.'

'—and found a recipe very similar to the one she'd been using to make the magic paint, except that it had an additional main ingredient. It used *kittens*.' Sybil paused while the cats in the audience let out little hisses. 'The witch who invented the spell first tried it using a fully grown cat, but the

218

cat just jumped out of the cauldron covered in gold liquid but unharmed. Then she realized that the difference between a kitten and an adult cat is that the kitten still contains a lot of growth potential. She guessed that the growth potential in a kitten might be an essential ingredient in the spell, so she decided to try it with a kitten instead. In fact, she recommended throwing in two at the same time for maximum effect!'

'And what happened when she did that?' Bunty demanded, glaring.

'There's a note written by the witch's daughter at the bottom of the page, saying that the result of the spell was a really splendid, large, gold cat but that the witch had been turned into a puff of green smoke.' She paused. 'Mother knew that I *could* harm a cat without the curse affecting me, so she sent me the spell and told me how to do it.

She *forced* me really.'

'I'm sure she had to force you very hard,' Bunty said sarcastically, 'since you're such a good-hearted person.'

Sybil looked sulky and didn't reply.

Bunty looked at the gold statue on the table. 'Do you know if there's any way of reversing this spell, Sybil?'

Sybil shook her head. 'Mother didn't say.'

'Then it looks like there's only one way to find out.' Bunty stood up. 'We shall have to call on Euphemia.'

At that, Doris quickly volunteered to be the one who stayed behind and got rid of all the kittens who were still cramming round the back door. The cats looked at her sharply when she said 'get rid of' and she swiftly added, 'Send them away, I mean.'

Bunty and Scarlett started to discuss the quickest way of getting to Euphemia's

house, and it was Scarlett who suggested they take Sybil's magic carpet. Bunty thought it was best if they left the gold statue behind with Felina to guard it. 'Any reversing spell is bound to involve using the same cauldron,' she explained, 'so the safest thing is to keep Mia here beside it.'

Felina gave a subdued mew in reply. She looked frightened, and India went over and rubbed her head against Felina's to comfort her once more before they left.

Cosmo had never been on a proper journey on a magic carpet before. Sybil was sitting between Scarlett and Bunty, so that the two witches could keep an eye on her, and Cosmo sat behind between his mother and father. He couldn't believe that they were really flying on *their* carpet from the garage. Cosmo found that he didn't feel as sick as when he was on the broomstick, apart from when the carpet

221

dipped then rose again suddenly to avoid a flock of birds.

India, after holding on tightly with her claws to begin with, was now starting to relax and enjoy herself. 'Why haven't you ever taken me flying with you before, Mephisto?' she asked Cosmo's father reproachfully. 'This is fun! Look at that black-bird! It's so close I could almost—'

'Don't!' said Mephisto, as she stretched out her paw. 'I don't want you falling off.' And he looked so irritated at the thought of her doing that, that she felt quite flattered and leaned forward to give his nose a lick.

'Mother's house is behind that row of trees just over there,' Sybil said after they had been flying for some time. She pointed to a house with a chimney that was painted green and purple. They landed in the front garden and the others held back as Bunty and Sybil went to knock on the front door.

Cosmo was starting to feel frightened now. Euphemia was a very powerful witch – possibly even more powerful than Bunty. What if she turned them all into frogs as soon as she saw them?

There was no reply, but the door was unlocked, so Bunty and Sybil went in.

'There's no sign of her,' Bunty called out, coming back to the front door after checking through all the rooms in the house.

Scarlett and the cats were amazed when

223

they stepped inside. Euphemia's home was totally decorated in gold. She had gold wallpaper, gold-coloured paint round her windows and gold carpets throughout. On the mantelpiece was the gold-cat statue that Euphemia had been showing off on the *Witch News*. Now they knew why its face seemed so lifelike.

Just looking at it made them all shiver.

'Where can she be?' Bunty muttered.

In a dark room at the back of the house, they found a lot of books.

'It's just like Professor Felina's study,' Cosmo said.

Bunty spotted a large book lying open on Euphemia's desk and when she went to look more closely, she saw that it was an ancient book of Dark Magic. Bunty had only seen a book like that once before, when she had accidently disturbed a very evil witch who was planning to use human babies in a spell to cure baldness. It was open at the page where the golden-cat recipe was written. Bunty read it very carefully.

The others watched as Bunty then flicked through the rest of the book until she came to a section at the back headed 'Reversing Spells'. She felt her heart beat faster as she came across the spell she was looking for. '*This spell will only work if done within two hours of the original spell*,' she read out loud. She looked up and said, 'So I'm afraid it's too late for that poor little kitten on the mantelpiece.'

'And it's nearly too late for Mia,' Scarlett said, checking her watch. 'We have to hurry, Aunt Bunty!'

Bunty frowned as she moved her finger down the list of ingredients. They seemed to be the same ones that had gone into the

225

original spell. Then she spotted one that was different. 'We need some fur from Mia's mother.'

India miaowed that that wouldn't be a problem. Felina would give up her whole fur coat if she thought it would save her kitten. Any mother cat would.

Bunty carried on reading, then nearly choked as she came to the next reversing-spell ingredient. 'It says we need to use one whole *witch*,' she gasped.

Everyone was silent, hardly able to believe that a witch would use another witch in a spell. Mephisto growled, feeling the hairs on his tail stand on end at the thought. He still felt very protective of witches in general, despite what he had discovered about Sybil.

'That's it then,' Scarlett said flatly. 'We can't do the spell. We can't save Mia.'

12

As everyone slowly took in this terrible news, Cosmo found himself staring up at the ceiling. Something was moving up there. It was hard to make out in the dark room, but Cosmo was almost sure it was a puff of green smoke.

He mewed to draw the others' attention to it, and when Bunty looked up she exclaimed, 'Of course!' as if something suddenly made sense to her now. 'It must have happened when Mia was turned to gold.'

'What are you talking about?' Sybil demanded.

'I wasn't sure how the curse worked,' Bunty continued, 'but now I can see that Doris was right to be afraid that if she didn't

227

do anything to help the kittens, the curse would apply to her too. Our ancestors have made sure that no witch can ever intentionally play *any* part in the death of a cat – even if the witch doesn't actually do the murder herself – without being lost as a smoke cloud.'

'Are you saying . . . ?' Sybil was staring up at the ceiling in disbelief. 'Are you saying, that's *Mother*?'

'I believe so,' Bunty replied, crisply.

Everyone was now staring in awe at the puff of green smoke above them, which had obviously become trapped in the room because all the windows were closed. Sybil started to call out her mother's name but everybody – including the puff of smoke – ignored her.

Bunty was looking thoughtful. 'I think I understand now. The spell needs one whole witch – but not necessarily in solid form.' She turned to her niece, beginning to sound more hopeful. 'Scarlett, go into the kitchen and see if you can find a large jar with a lid on it.'

She began to search down the rest of the list, stopping as she found the last ingredient

229

that they needed for the reversing spell. 'It says that the final thing to go in must be a witch-cat sneeze – but it has to be from a cat who was born under the same star as Mia.'

Cosmo turned excitedly to his mother. 'I know all about the stars! Father told me! One star always shines extra brightly on the night you're born, and that's how you know which star to join when you die.'

'That's correct,' India replied, exchanging a smile with Mephisto. 'And that is the same for *all* cats, not just witch-cats. All mother cats know which star their kittens were born under.'

'Will Mia's mother know which star *she* was born under then?' Cosmo asked, but before India could answer he continued, 'Because if Mia was born under the same star as me, I could use one of *my* sneezes to make her come back again, couldn't I?'

Cosmo's whiskers were standing right out from his face, twitching excitedly.

At that moment Bunty, who had climbed up on to the table to reach the ceiling, succeeded in capturing the green puff of smoke in the jar Scarlett had brought her from the kitchen. 'Got you!' she gasped, screwing the lid back on as tightly as she could. She turned and looked down at the others. 'Now . . . let's get back to Mia and see what we can do!'

They found Felina sitting with her tail wrapped around herself for comfort, staring miserably at the gold statue. She jumped up when they came in, giving Sybil a hiss to warn her to keep as far away from her as possible. Prison was too good for Sybil as far as Felina was concerned.

'Felina, we've found a spell that might

231

change Mia back again, but we have to act quickly,' Bunty said, looking at the kitchen clock. The whole trip to Euphemia's house and back had taken over an hour, and Sybil had told them that she had put Mia in the cauldron at least half an hour before they had arrived. That meant that the two hours had to be almost up. 'Firstly, I'll need some of your loose hairs.'

Since cats always shed a lot of hair when they are nervous, there was plenty coming off Felina's coat now.

'Good,' said Bunty, gathering up a whole handful. 'We have the puff of witch right here. But as for the magic sneeze . . .' She looked at the cats. 'I'll have to leave that to you.'

'Felina, what star was Mia born under?' India asked urgently.

'The brightest one of course.'

'Different stars are the brightest on different nights,' India reminded her, thinking that Felina wasn't sounding like her normal professor-self at all. 'We have to know which one shone the brightest when Mia was born.'

Felina frowned. 'Well . . . I could point to it, if it was night-time, or I could tell you the name that the ancient Greeks gave it—'

'Was it a big yellow star with a circle of smaller stars around it?' India asked impatiently.

'Yes,' Felina nodded, but just as India was getting excited and saying that it must be the same star as Cosmo's, Felina seemed to snap back into being a professor again. 'Not necessarily, India. That description fits many different stars. In my book on astronomy there are at least—'

'We haven't got much time!' Bunty

233

reminded them, looking anxiously at the clock.

India frowned at her friend. 'There isn't time to go and look at your astronomy book now, Felina.' She paused. 'My *instincts* tell me that Cosmo and Mia must have been born under the same star. Cats who pair up together nearly always are.' She was thinking of Mephisto and herself, who had both been born under a lone white star, which shone most brightly in the winter months. 'Doesn't your gut tell you that too?'

'It's just that . . .' Felina broke off, agitated. It was just that normally she never acted on her gut feelings until she had searched her books thoroughly for evidence to support them. But she knew as well as India that there was no time for that now. 'Yes,' she mewed finally. 'It does.'

Mephisto, who had been waiting nearby,

miaowed for Cosmo to begin climbing the steps of the cauldron. Bunty, seeing that the cats were ready, picked up the golden statue and carefully lowered it back inside the magic liquid. Everyone watched silently as she threw in the handful of Felina's loose fur, then took the jar with the puff of witch inside, and plunged it deep into the cauldron liquid. With her free hand she unscrewed the lid, and immediately a hissing sound came from under the surface as if a snake was swimming round and round very fast before disappearing into nothing.

Bunty removed the empty jar and stood back. Now it was Cosmo's turn. He was at the top of the cauldron steps now. Scarlett had the pepper pot ready for him.

He sniffed hard until the inside of his nose felt ticklish. 'A-A-A-TISHOO!' he burst out, sending a huge shower of magic

235

sneeze into the cauldron.

The noise that followed nearly made him fall off the steps. There was a bang, louder than any bang Cosmo had heard before, then the surface of the liquid seemed to explode into a fountain of gold stars. And then something even stranger happened. The stars stopped being gold in colour and changed to what could only be described as *tabby* coloured.

As the stars kept shooting up into the air, ripples started to appear on the surface of the cauldron liquid. Cosmo leaned forward without thinking, and as a star collided with his gold paw, there was a loud hiss and his fur started to tingle. Cosmo pulled his paw away quickly, then miaowed in excitement as a familiar tabby-coloured head surfaced inside the cauldron amidst a lot of coughing and splashing.

Bunty rushed forward to rescue Mia, and a few minutes later, the kitten was lying on the floor and Felina was purring with relief and licking every part of her daughter over and over, just as she had done when she had first given birth to her.

Cosmo was racing round and round the room, too excited to stand still.

'Cosmo, come here!' Mia called out to him.

Cosmo went over to her, his tail still bushy with adrenalin. Mia was about to speak when her eyes fell on his paw. 'Oh,' she exclaimed, because it was no longer golden.

'Oh no!' Cosmo gasped, seeing that his right front paw was now tabby coloured.

'*I* think it looks very handsome,' Mia said quickly. 'And anyway, *I* like you, no matter what colour your paws are!'

All Cosmo's skin started to tingle, not because it was changing colour again, but because that was the nicest thing Mia had ever said to him – and he forgot all about his paw as he gave the top of her head a big wet lick in reply.

13

Cosmo and Mia were lying in Sybil's front garden a few evenings later, gazing up at the sky.

'That's our star up there,' Cosmo said, pointing up at a bright-yellow star with his paw.

Mia looked up at it. 'Mother's going to teach me the names of all the stars next week,' she said. 'This week we're doing planets.' Mia had become more enthusiastic about her mother's lessons since she had learned how to spell the word TUNA in crunchy-munchies. That was her favourite thing to eat, and Amy never seemed to buy any. Amy had responded by buying in a large supply of the stuff and inviting all her friends round to see the letters (which they all refused to believe had been put there by her cats).

Cosmo didn't seem to be listening very hard. He was staring at a board that had been erected in front of Sybil's house that afternoon. The board belonged to one of the local estate agents – Witch Properties R Us – and it was invisible to the human eye. It was advertising the house as being available for sale immediately.

'I wonder who'll move in next,' Cosmo said. 'They might not want us to stay. They might have their own witch-cat.'

'I couldn't bear it if you had to move away,' Mia mewed. 'Couldn't you move in with us instead?'

Cosmo didn't think he could stand to live in the same house as the professor cat and be made to do lessons every day – but he didn't want to hurt Mia's feelings by saying that. So

241

instead he said, 'I don't think we could. Father says we have to live with another witch.'

At that moment, Mephisto was lying stretched out on Sybil's bed watching India twist herself up in the purple bedroom curtains.

'I really like living inside a house,' she told him. India had moved inside from the garage as soon as Sybil had been taken away. 'But I wouldn't have liked it when Sybil was here.'

Mephisto just grunted. He still couldn't think of Sybil – and all the years of calling her 'mistress' – without his fur standing on end.

'What's wrong, Mephisto?' India asked.

A tight growl sounded in the back of Mephisto's throat. 'How could I have been so easily deceived? Even my own kitten realized the truth sooner than I did.'

India unwrapped herself from her make-believe sari and jumped up on to the bed beside him. 'You mustn't blame yourself. You can't help being so powerful that even a non-witch seems like she has magic powers in your presence.' She gave his ear a lick.

Mephisto frowned. He hadn't thought of it quite like that before. 'It's true that I can't *help* being almost one hundred per cent witch-cat,' he agreed.

'Exactly,' India purred. 'Mephisto, there's something else I wanted to—'

But before she could continue, something flew past their window that made them both leap off the bed.

It was Bunty and Scarlett on their magic carpet, and by the time India and Mephisto got downstairs, Cosmo and Mia were already

243

rubbing themselves against the witches'
ankles and purring loudly in welcome.

'I went to visit the witch prison today,'
Bunty told them. 'Sybil's not going to
have an easy time there. The first
thing they did when she arrived
was a "Finding Out" spell!'

'What's that?' India,
Cosmo and Mia all

mewed together, and Bunty seemed to understand them because she continued, 'It's a spell that can be done to find out all the things you secretly hate the most. They did it on Sybil, and now she's got to have Brussels sprouts, boiled cabbage and very lumpy tapioca pudding to eat every day, and she has to wear a pink, frilly dress with matching knickers and pink shoes with big bows on the front.' Bunty smiled at the thought of it. 'She gets let out of prison to help others during the day, because helping others is what she hates doing most of all. This week they've got her helping old ladies to cross the road in the mornings and removing fleas from local cats in the afternoons. And she can't run away because they've tagged her with an electronic tag, so that if she tries to escape, the prison warden can locate where she is straight away and

245

turn her into a frog. Oh, and she's not allowed to watch any television. She's very upset about that!'

All four cats miaowed their approval.

But Bunty had more to tell them. 'Now that Sybil won't be needing her house any longer and it's been put up for sale, I was wondering . . . how would you like it if my sister, Goody, moved in here with her family?'

Scarlett broke in breathlessly. 'It was my idea! Mum and Dad still haven't found a witch's house that they like in the country, and I think *this* house would be perfect!'

'You must all carry on living here too, of course,' Bunty said. 'Goody's witch-cat has just retired to Cornwall, because he thinks the weather is better down there, and she's been looking for a cat to replace him.'

Cosmo couldn't believe it! He was so happy that he started to run round the

246

garden, his tail bushed up with excitement. He loved the idea of living in the same house as Scarlett – and he and Mia could still see each other every day.

Mephisto gave a satisfied miaow. He was pleased as well. It would be a relief to work with a proper witch again.

'And, India, you must live in the house with us from now on!' Scarlett added. 'Mum says that *all* cats should be treated like part of the family – not just witch-cats!'

India, who had sat down and begun to wash herself, said, 'I should think so. I have no intention of spending another winter in that draughty garage after the kittens arrive.'

'*What* kittens?' Cosmo and Mephisto asked in astonishment.

But India just looked very pleased with herself, gave her tummy a lick, and purred.

Also by Gwyneth Rees

Connie has never believed in fairies, so she is amazed when Ruby, a tiny fairy-girl, suddenly appears in the library of the old house where Connie is staying.

Ruby says that she is a book fairy – but that she is in terrible trouble. She has been banished from fairyland until she finds a ruby ring, which she has lost.

Can Connie help Ruby find the missing ring – before the doorway to fairyland is closed forever?